I, Gabriel

Dominic Holland

ISBN: 978-1-999765-61-3 (paperback)

ACKNOWLEDGEMENTS

I must thank my good friend, the talented and kind Marcus Landau of Conker Design (www.conkerdesign.co.uk) for designing the jacket for this novel and also the jacket for *Eclipsed.*

It was Marcus's idea to create a CD of my stand-up show, *Dominic Holland is Alive in Tring.* It should be said that selling these CDs has been difficult. In fact, it is almost impossible to even give them away and yet I bear him no ill-will and we remain good friends. That said, he's under water and *I,Gabriel* seriously needs to shift…

Thank you to all of my early readers for their encouragement and pointers. In no particular order… Helen, Helen, Ray, Dr. Gary Colman, Nikki, Heidi, Lawrence, Catherine, Windsor, Sarah, Suzanne, Liz and Mike.

To Nikki for her patience as I write another blinking novel. Her question, "Dom, can we afford for you to write another book?" is a good one and time will tell.

To my new friend Raef Meeuwisse, my go-to man for all things on-line publishing. We met at a conference in Germany that I was hosting and Raef was an expert/keynote speaker. How he must rue the moment he thought to approach the conference host. A costly compliment indeed.

INTRODUCTION

Hello, my name is Gabriel Webber.

I am many things in life, including a boobs man which is a dangerous admission but there are reasons for such candour and will become clear soon enough.

I should not be here. By rights, I should be dead and yet I don't feel blessed or fortunate for being spared. The sounds ungrateful, I know and for this I feel ashamed.

As I write, I am in a heightened state of excitement but also deep sadness and anxiety. In truth, I am lost. I am looking to find my way again and I hope that you might accompany me.

Really, I should begin with an apology: that I am not a writer and nor do I know what this is. A novel perhaps, an essay, a piece of journalism or even a case study. I do not know and I do not particularly care since it is not so important. What is important however is this story; a story I have no option but to tell. A book I am compelled to write. I would have preferred if it could have been written for me in the way that other (great) lives are chronicled. Not that I am so lazy, although this is a factor, but more because I am not a man of words. I did enquire about hiring a scribe, but after meeting a few charlatans I realised that my instincts were correct and that I must write it myself. There is another more curious reason why I must be at the helm, but more of this later and throughout. In truth, I haven't all the answers myself as yet and I am hoping for enlightenment as I write. A catharsis for me then and, I hope, for us all.

I hope so, as, I write what I suppose is my autobiography. By any comparisons it is an extraordinary life and doing it justice is a formidable challenge. A task made more onerous since I am writing in the first person and by modern standards, I am afraid that I am not a very likeable man.

It is an advantage for any story if the hero and narrator is relatable and likeable; easy to admire? This is not the case here. Although people admire me, they do not like me. I know this because, the internet being what it is, they tell me. I am a man of great accomplishments but matched by my failings, all of which must be exposed if this book is to serve any real purpose for me and for my readers.

I used to have quirks and idiosyncrasies which were considered comic, but not any longer. This partly explains why I need to write this introduction. With modern sensitivities as they are, it can serve as a confession - but also a warning.

So, let this introduction serve also as a plea; to encourage my more delicate readers to set aside their pre-judgements so that they can complete this short but important work. It saved my life and I hope that it can save yours too. I am aware that this is some claim. And whilst I do have a highly refined sense of self and am prone to melodrama, I am not being dramatic in this instance, as you are about to discover.

You have my assurances that I will write with fearless honesty. A confessional of a brilliant but flawed man. Anything less is a waste of all our time. Fitting, too, because I consider it to be the greatest accomplishment in my esteemed life. My indelible mark on the world. Isn't this what we all strive for?

As with anything worth achieving, writing a book is not an easy task. It requires much effort and courage and time is against me. These are troubled times and the moral of this story and its timing are prescient. Another lofty claim. Setting myself up to fail, perhaps? Well, read on and decide for yourself.

Someone once said, 'never explain, nor apologise'. I don't like this sentiment but I agree with it, although I concede that I have explained myself already in this introduction. However, I will not be apologising. Inevitably some will accuse me of being motivated by the income that accompanies a best-selling book, but I refute this. Even in my admission that avarice is my central failing and the kernel of this story, financial gain is not at play here. Something higher is at work which I have a heavy burden to understand and to share. The strong international sales and bountiful income (plus, no doubt, the film rights), whilst most welcome, are merely a bonus and almost a distraction.

This is a true story. A modern-day parable, worthy of Jesus Christ himself. Plenty of pretenders since then have laid claim to the second coming but not me. I am not God. I am just an ordinary man. Well, perhaps not so ordinary.

Finally, I will write with economy so that the message can quickly emerge. Less is more and ever more so as our attention spans diminish.

I, Gabriel is my gift to the world. No need to thank me. But do, please, tell your friends and loved ones.

CHAPTER ONE

I am unsure when this story properly starts nor where I should begin. May 4th this year, seven months ago now, is certainly pivotal and January 12th this year also. But really these dates, although prominent, are mere punctuation marks in a much larger story that I am striving to understand.

As I write, it is a cold December evening and I am resident in a modest London hotel, having left my beautiful Georgian double fronted villa with its two-car garage, a walled garden with a tennis court in the heart of Marylebone village. The reasons for this will become clear as I account for my life and how it has come to all but collapse.

I am blessed with many things in life and perhaps most obviously, my wealth. Too often, wealth is confused with success. A primary school teacher can achieve great things and be an extraordinary success and yet in financial terms is flat average and therefore a failure?

I am fortunate that I am both. I am incredibly successful and spectacularly wealthy. It is also noteworthy that I am a self-made millionaire – and a millionaire in the old-fashioned sense of the word; when being a 'millionaire' meant something and denoted real wealth. These days a millionaire is practically anyone who happens to own a drab four-bed semi in Hendon, or somewhere else as tired. And whilst it is vulgar to boast about wealth, it is a part of who I am and central to my story.

Wealth and riches are relative of course. The disparities between 'haves' and 'have nots' being the fertile plains on which politicians and other power brokers make their hay. Nor are matters of wealth inequity helped by gauging poverty in comparative terms; since we are all paupers by comparison with someone else and illogical since the poorest people today in the 'developed' world are wealthier than practically all their predecessors. And it seems we are no happier for our vastly increased riches.

If social scientists are to be believed, it seems that mankind is becoming progressively more anxious and less happy. It appears the people who foraged and didn't see their thirties lived happier lives than modern man, who spends his (on average) eight decades in a heated home with running water, flushing toilets, self-cleaning ovens, coffee machines, broadband and other modern marvels.

Since mankind has never had so much 'stuff', it follows then that happiness is not a factor of material wealth. This is hardly revelatory, but could it be that our burgeoning possessions are making us unhappy?

The cliché has it that money cannot buy happiness and yet money is what we are innately programmed to strive for. More money to acquire more stuff. The newest, biggest, smallest, fastest… in a never-ending cycle of dizzy despair.

Well, I am truly blessed then, since by any gauge, I am wealthy and I was also happy until an abrupt awakening obliterated my perfect and smug equation and I find myself in this hotel with only my computer for company. I am not happy at all. I am desolate and might even commit suicide if I didn't have this story to share. A lifesaving book then in so many ways.

Loneliness is central to my unhappiness. I have few friends and no one to confide in and my isolation is compounded by feeling marginalised by the modern world. I am completely bewildered by modern thinking. I agree with almost nothing said by anyone under the age of thirty-five, or by people my own age but who refer to themselves as 'progressive'. This is important because it is these two groups who set the agenda and wield the power. These are the arbiters and the architects of society and, whether intentionally or not in my not so humble opinion, they are making a dog's dinner of it.

I recall the recent passing of Professor Stephen Hawking and his painful, distorted face staring out from every newspaper and world media outlet. If ever there was a victim who had no time for victimhood. Hawking's life is a remarkable one. A life, not so curtailed in its length as was predicted, but certainly blighted by his wretched disease and yet he lived his life to its full potential and without even a whiff of 'why me'. By modern standards this is a remarkable achievement and, I think, might even be this great man's greatest feat.

But the likes of Steven Hawking are literally dying off, replaced by a generation who are being schooled in the new artform of victimhood. Never in the history of mankind have so many people been so offended by so little. This sentence itself is offensive for its use of the word 'mankind', which the current Prime Minister of Canada has suggested we should avoid. What chance is there for our race when such craven individuals are able to become our leaders?

Today offense does not need to be explained nor accounted for but merely asserted. A pernicious, sinister development; not least because it undermines genuine victims and their suffering, but most damaging because it absolves people of any personal responsibility for their behaviour and outcomes.

'It's not my fault' is the common refrain, implying then that someone else is to blame. Parents. Schools. Teachers. The police. The government, or society more generally?

Victimhood has been granted value and as such, has become something worth pursuing. A dangerous development and a folly and any group pursuing it unintentionally disadvantages itself; a sanctioned form of self-harm.

Martin Luther King's great speech fell on deaf ears. He

would be aghast that identity is now less to do with one's character and everything to do with which group we belong to. Male, female and now a myriad other genders. Race, sexuality, class and so it goes on, making it impossible for anyone to keep up.

Nowadays I find myself in many groups which I feel a need to apologise for. I am old. White. Rich. Male. Judeo-Christian. Heterosexual. These are not groups that I have joined, they are just who I am and how I was born. They are immutable. I can renounce Christianity, but this does not alter my ancestry. And although I can now identify as a female, whatever these clever surgeons can remove from or append to my body, I will remain as I was born, a man. An irrefutable fact and yet somehow this is now a scandalous statement and possibly even a crime.

As lonely as I am, it is peculiar then that I don't court more popular views. Belligerence perhaps and no matter how many 'experts' line up against me. Most recently I have fallen foul of the increasingly empowered and strident women's movement, so easily done nowadays - just ask the eminent Germaine Greer. To think that as a student, I proudly marched with my sisters calling for equality and with such success; women now heading up countries, police forces and corporations. But at what cost, since it seems that modern feminism is most effective now at making ordinary women feel miserable. And these waters are made even more treacherous by the aforementioned trans-movement, which has taken many by surprise and strikes most people dumb with fear as feminists and men identifying as women increasingly rage at each other.

The ascent of the trans-movement is remarkable, gaining full accreditation with their own letter T grafted on to make the acronym LGBT. A stunning victory by co-opting the energies and guile of the battle-hardened gay lobby with more time on their hands now since they have won their arguments so handsomely. And good for them.

By occupying the moral high ground, the trans arguments are impregnable because detractors, even as esteemed and seemingly qualified as Martina Navratilova can be cast aside as immoral or cruel. Add to this the protection of the law, since hate crimes are now a reality. But isn't hate subjective with degrees and nuances? And who decides? Our esteemed lawyers? But the law is not a science. It is interpretative and there is no shortage of avaricious lawyers hunting down the offended to nobly defend them. Or feed off them?

A rotten system then, serving mainly the professionals within and immune to any common sense and even facts which explains how the unequivocal science of biology has been trumped by the new science of sociology.

A mother in labour, in the throes of agony and ecstasy as her baby is being born. Naturally, she wants to know if it is healthy and what sex it is. But who knows these days? Dunno, time will tell. This baby can be whatever it chooses to be? A position helped along by craven celebrities allowing their offspring to choose. In which case, my advice is that they should choose another set of blinking parents and quickly.

This edifice crumbles soon enough when opportunists use the same logic to change their race and even their age. Or male prisoners claiming womanhood to be housed in female jails so that they can continue the sex crimes for which they are imprisoned. Male candidates on all female shortlists and male athletes winning female sports events. A journeyman male tennis player might as well hitch up a skirt and win women's Wimbledon, taking home the equal pay cheque for such light work.

Not that there are not gender anomalies, although thankfully these are rare. Babies born with both genitalia and none. Hermaphrodites and androgyny. These are tragedies, but the plight of these few is made worse by the similar claims of the many. And so, confronting such orthodoxies is to protect the weak and the vulnerable, no? And yet, for doing so I am somehow the monster.

I expect I have lost a raft of readers already, many of whom are now reaching for their devices in order to send me their invective.

Online is the battlefield where the 'justice warriors' go to war. Emboldened by anonymity and mutual support, they seek out the slightest dissent and they attack. Very often, I am called a 'Nazi', which is particularly hollow since my wife is Jewish and her grandparents and extended family were killed by these repugnant people. I made this point on Twitter in response to an account called @alljewsarenazis and got in return not an apology, but a simple one-word response. 'Good'. How charming.

But enough of what is wrong with the world. What of the man, Gabriel Webber, you will be wanting to know. I have been married to Judith for almost thirty years and we have no children. Not a loveless marriage, but one that is certainly bloody tired. Limp, but reasonably happy and practically functional.

I am fifty-five years old and by 'boobs man' I am referring to my career as a breast surgeon. This revelation might demonstrate my poor sense of humour rather more than assuage any offence caused earlier. Well done to those readers who were offended but are still with me. Hastily, I must explain that I no longer refer to myself as such. I might be insensitive but I am not stupid. On the contrary, I am brilliant and officially so if IQ scores are to be believed. I did, however, used to introduce myself this way. At parties, it was my thing.

'Hello. Gabriel Webber. I'm a boobs man. You?'

Any raised eyebrows would quickly relax on my jokey reveal, receiving laughter from both men and women as well as requests for my business card. Happy days indeed but now, long gone. And to think I could have been more vulgar given the innumerable names for the female breast. Bosoms of course. Baps. Jugs. Hooters. Tits. Melons. Bristol's… you get my point. I argue that they all contribute to the great allure and majesty of the female breast.

Time for a break?

A chance to give my readers pause for thought. But do please stick with me. I have much wisdom and enlightenment to impart.

CHAPTER TWO

To the 12th January 2018 then, a watershed in my life courtesy of the Financial Times which ran an article with the headline:

Famed, Millionaire Breast Surgeon Dares to Lecture Women on Pay.

The shock aside, I was initially relaxed by this. If anything, I was quite flattered; 'famed' no less, albeit being a mere 'millionaire' grated a little. The whole thing was a set-up which I should have seen coming, but perhaps my ego intervened.

Trolls are aptly named. They might be few in number but they wield immense power. Permanently aggrieved, their fury is something to behold and, like a shoal of piranhas, they devoured me.

I should explain why a newspaper set out to throw a surgeon under the bus. I blame lots of people for this. The editors and the journalist. The trolls of course and their faux offence, but ahead of all these people, I blame our sociologists.

Sociology: study of development, structure and functioning of human society.

Think back to your school days and recall the very cleverest kids in your class. The elite children who breezed through school. It is likely that they entered the professions; doctors, lawyers or accountants; and that a few mavericks amongst them became entrepreneurs. No doubt also some will have flunked and never fulfilled their promise. But it is unlikely that many of them became sociologists. Very bright children have options and rarely is sociology on their radars. So, if sociologists are the thinkers who shape our society, it follows then that we are being moulded by the comparatively stupid.

Modern thinking has framed society in to an adversarial model where myriad groups are pitted against one another. No bad thing perhaps, since it is a human race with the survival of the fittest. But this new order relies on confected and faux rivalries, thriving on discord and acrimony, and nowhere is this more evident than in the battle of the sexes.

This needn't be a battle, of course. For millennia men and women have co-existed with remarkable success due to a natural synergy of combined and complimentary skills.

...Dr. Webber is the acceptable face of institutional prejudice. He represents an insidious wing of the patriarchy and is legitimised by his vaunted profession, but he is an unreconstructed misogynist, countering the progress that is demanded by decent, modern and progressive people...

Financial Times, 12th January 2018

There is much for me to dwell on in this excerpt: 'institutional', 'progressive', 'patriarchy' and finally, 'misogynist'. All words that are relatively new and specifically conceived for this phoney war and I refute them all being aimed at me.

Misogyny: feelings of hating women, or the belief that men are much better than women.

Certainly, misogyny does occur. In too many places around the world women are dealt a lowly and appalling hand. Girls are aborted, discarded or maimed as beggars. Female genital mutilation. Forced marriage. Incestuous marriage. Sex slavery.

And yet such grave realities do not exorcise the mob who reserve their ire for a breast surgeon with a sense of mischief.

I happen to love women; a statement now frowned upon because of what else it implies: creepiness, philandering and misogyny. But female beauty is my expertise and where my fortune is founded. A beautiful woman is attractive. People admire beauty and are attracted to it and which explains why it is so desirable. Beauty is a true blessing and why people, women in particular, spend so much time and money pursuing it.

But female beauty is a distraction now from the modern feminist cause. Women's beauty is objectifying and it detracts from other characteristics of the modern woman. But not, however, the female characteristics and traits that are so apparent, well developed and vital. Characteristics like kindness, nurture, patience, maternity, empathy, sensitivity, generosity, warmth, loyalty and a profound capacity for love. These soft skills are crucial and form the bedrock on which any civilized and successful society thrives. These nuanced skills are instinctive. They cannot be taught. They are innate and they are more abundant in females because they are crucial for motherhood which whatever my medical colleagues claim they can achieve, will always be the preserve of women. Which so happens to be the most important role in society and why women are venerated and yet, to the progressives, this is a heresy and a threat; just another part of the patriarchy and men's subjugation of women.

Accordingly, sociologists state that such traits are not innate. They are learned. They are societal. They are characteristics imposed on girls by wicked men with cruel intentions.

In the new world order, men and women are the same; both as capable as each other and in all areas of endeavour. Total nonsense to anyone sane and rational. Current understanding is that everything is learned. Nurture not nature. Boys and girls are the same. Blank canvasses. Maternal feelings are not innate. A mother does not feel a greater bond with her child than a father. Gestating the child within her body, giving birth and then lactating creates no greater bond with the child than is felt by the father, who might have already scarpered after a knee-trembler in a pub car park. Famous and rich women can now sub-out gestation to poor surrogates and it is somehow a reasonable thing to do.

And for this social construct to be fully complete, it follows that women must lay claim to other characteristics like strength, bravery, cunning, competitiveness, toughness, grit, ambition and ruthlessness. Traits more easily associated with men. Before such engineering the very obvious differences between men and women were not an issue because the sexes co-existed and indeed, depended on each other. That word synergy again. It is how we evolved.

Carol

John, do you think you and your mates can kill that hairy bison over there?

John

Dunno, why?

Carol

Because I reckon it will be good to eat.

John

You think?

Carol

Yeah, if I cook it on this fire. And we could even make clothes from its hide.

John

What's a hide?

Carol

Just go and kill it.

John

Well, hang on a moment. That's easy for you to say. It's huge and...

Carol

And after we've eaten it, I will fuck your brains out...

And with this John and his mates grab their spears, intoxicated by the idea of a full stomach but mostly of getting laid. Whichever God is yours, it cannot be denied that men and women are designed for one another. An irrefutable reality and unfortunate truth if factoring in any hurt this might cause to people not so wired.

But this co-existence is no longer needed. Increasingly, women proclaim that they no longer need men, because needing men implies weakness and fallibility. Marriage is being consigned to history because it implies ownership. Semen is available online along with an array of dildos. Ironically, men are fucked. Their time is over. A bad thing for women and a disaster for society, since men have proven to be so very good at certain tasks, for instance building things like roads, ships, canals, sewers, railways, trains, aeroplanes...

Men and women are definitely not the same. But we are not meant to be because we are complimentary. On average, men are stronger and bigger than women. Of course, some women are stronger than some men. But the strongest woman is not as strong as the strongest man, nor as big or as fast or as durable. Why else do women not complete the cycling tours that men do? And why are equality professionals not scandalised by this and demand to know why the Williams sisters are not playing five sets?

And finally, women are more beautiful than men. From Aphrodite to Marilyn Monroe and any number of women venerated today, female beauty is absolute and led me in to my trap by the Financial Times.

'...the views of a dinosaur, he belongs to a by-gone age and we can take solace that more enlightened times are ahead...'

The Financial Times, 12th January, 2018

I was invited to give a lecture on ethics and morals at the London School of Economics. Naturally my speech leant heavily on my professional expertise. The beauty industry in the US alone is worth over $500 billion per annum, eighty percent of which is accounted for by women.

'Yes, dickhead! Spent by women, but why? For whom? For men! You stupid, horrible man. There's a patriarchy, don't you know?'

This is one of the politer comments from an online comments board that followed the newspaper feature and I found impossible to ignore.

This is a common repost to the reality that women are interested in beauty only because they are objectified by men, who happen to run the world - hence the shrill calls to end such slavery and beautification. In the past, women have appeared on red carpets without make-up or heels but the craze never lasts very long because, the awkward truth is, women really do like beauty.

At the hallowed university during the customary question and answers after my speech, the thorny issue of pay inequality was raised and I decided to be a little mischievous. To give a little context, my speech had not been well received and I had recognised the wage gap question for what it was: a noose and I was happy to pop my head through. A murmur of approval had spread through the hall and the place hung heavy in anticipation which I had rather savoured, even pausing for effect.

"I assume by your question you are referring to the iniquitous situation whereby a man earns more money than a woman for the same role or function?" I began confidently. The hall waited, sensing that my crucial qualification was about to arrive. My questioner had purple hair, hideous tattoos and was the size of an expensive fridge. Her colleagues sat ready to pounce, like greyhounds in their traps ahead of a race, pressed against the grills, desperate for the latch to spring and their chance to tear at their prey.

"And this, of course, is quite wrong..." I continued as the hounds bared their teeth and the occasional impatient head smashed against the gate; every muscle and sinew straining, waiting for their chance. I was not about to disappoint.

"...were it to occur"

The crowd was impatient now. All heads smashing into gates, the disquiet in the room, audible.

"Because for a function or a role that can be accurately metered and, as importantly, measured; a supermarket check-out machine for instance,' I continued slowly, choosing my words carefully, 'this is quite wrong and it must be that anyone performing such a duty, be it male or female, must be paid the same. And is a legal requirement."

Come on you old dinosaur. Get to the point. Get to the BUT. There's always a BUT with these cunts. We know it's coming and when it does...

"But..." I uttered. The relief was palpable. Like a rusty screw finally giving up its fight.

"...but, in roles where output and value are more subjective and nuanced, I can see situations where different sexes will realise different levels of income and this is quite proper."

There were audible huffs at this. I was warming to my task as the metaphorical stuffed hare began its second unimpeded lap of the track.

"Perhaps I can demonstrate my point. Due to the greater market size and the vastly bigger dollar revenues that they create, it is entirely appropriate that male models should make a paltry income compared to their female colleagues."

And with that old chestnut, they came at me. Who let the dogs out, as the famous lyric goes. As one they pounced and I could not add to my argument. Female actors in the adult film industry? Or female actors in Hollywood, depending on star size and draw? But alas, the place exploded and I needed to be escorted from the building. It was all pretty thrilling. I felt like a rock star holed up in the staff room as the mob pressed against the door and chanted their abuse. Eventually PC Plod arrived and no prizes for guessing whose side he took, fresh from his inclusivity away days and seminars.

But I hadn't expected the press coverage nor the hideous aftermath which I came to regret. It put an end to my speaking engagements which I rather enjoyed and would be a most welcome distraction for me now.

Polly Wales was the FT journalist and I felt compelled to look her up. A privately educated, middle class girl who I shouldn't imagine has struggled for much in life and yet makes a living out of grievance.

...and given his renown academic prowess, it is a great shame and rather telling that he should apply his abilities to this somewhat tawdry area of medicine...

The Financial Times, Jan 12th 2018

This easy accusation is common and always rankles. As a cosmetic breast surgeon, I must forego the beatification that other doctors enjoy which is irksome but a price worth paying. A common accusation is that I have sold out. That my patients are merely customers. Which is true, but so what? Patients? Customers? Punters? It's all the same. People with cancer are the customers of drugs companies, no? And such companies who invest billions to discover new drugs are driven by profits and not cures or altruism.

Another accusation is that I am not treating the sick, but what is unhappiness if not an ailment? My patients are almost always unhappy and they believe that I can help alleviate it. I can't, but this is their concern and not mine and why my psychiatrist colleagues are on-hand once this realisation occurs.

Soon after I received a strident letter from the Vice-Chancellor of the LSE explaining the grave offence I had caused. She went on to explain that I would not be welcomed to speak at the university again and added that this was likely to extend to other campuses as well. Blackballed in my day, no platformed today. I did a cursory internet search on the pompous academic and was pleasantly surprised by her striking good looks; no doubt a factor in her success and another observation that is best not made these days…

The On-line hate soon became more real and tangible with a bunch of incandescent protestors arriving outside my surgery with banners variously describing me as a pig and a butcher. Patients cancelled their appointments but the protesters eventually got bored and moved on, most likely onto another easy and pointless target. My practice quickly recovered and brings me to another crucial date in this story, 4th May 2018 and my final examination of a patient called Bella.

CHAPTER THREE

Bella is not her real name. I cannot provide her real name because I do not know it. Bella is twenty-six years old and I imagine is quite the world beauty. I imagine this because I have never seen her face. She is one of the many wives or consorts of a man who has already settled her bill, for which I am most grateful. Although I have never met this man, he is one of my most loyal and valuable clients; Bella being the sixth patient that he has sent to me for a touch-up, or 'refurb' shall we say.

My work does have a clandestine feel to it. For obvious reasons, my 'patients' demand absolute discretion and prefer to let God take the credit for their shapely form. Flick through any magazine of the rich and famous and my work is there to be admired. The world's most 'beautiful' women are my clients. The subtle line through a ballgown or a bulging bikini on a Dubai beach are my great works. As demanding as it is to become a word class surgeon, for a man as vain as I am, keeping these things quiet is the hardest element of my job. A good thing then that I am so well remunerated.

Bella is accompanied by her two female assistants and a male bodyguard. All three of the women are wearing full face veils. Although I am used to this, it remains a peculiar reality that Bella is sitting opposite me with her breasts exposed and yet I am not allowed to see her face. Her bodyguard is facing the wall and daren't turn around for what could be a career ending glimpse. Other than me, the only man who gets to see my work is the man paying for it and presumably he gets to see her face as well? A colleague of mine, a surgeon in Santa Monica, has seen Bella's face because he did her lips, and he tells me that she is a flat out ten.

"Now, you mean?" I had asked him, and he roared with laughter.

"Any pain?" I ask Bella as I gently press her perfectly shaped left breast. I cup it with my gloved hand and gently take the weight.

"Does that feel okay? Any pain at all, or any tightness?"

Bella stares straight ahead and, after a moment of consideration, she barely nods her head and I am pleased. No pain is excellent news and they certainly feel and appear to be in great shape. I should imagine that his excellency is in for hours of fun and a decent return on his investment.

"Good. And are you happy with the results?" I ask, ever happy to receive praise.

Bella doesn't reply and I don't push. It's not for her to say, I suppose. If he is not happy then I will learn soon enough. Over the years I have noticed that his tastes have moderated to reflect the changes in fashion; nowadays preferring smaller, more pert breasts and, most recently, plenty of flank breast tissue since 'side boob' has become such a thing which dress designers have been quick to herald. Like all his previous wives or mistresses, I have darkened Bella's areola using the original shade card that he provided and I have also coaxed the nipples to stand erect and proud whether stimulated or not. No pressure on him then.

The account is already settled in full, as is a strict policy of mine. Excellent value at twenty grand each. Plus, VAT, which I dutifully collect on behalf of Her Majesty's government. Surely a gong can't be too far off for all the money I have raised for my country?

Bella has now finished her course of medication and so

today I am signing her off. The private jet will be waiting and presumably so too, his excellency.

"Well I am very pleased with the results, Bella." I stand up to signal the end of the consultation. My work is done and we both have flights to catch. I strip off my gloves and begin rolling down my shirt sleeves as I wait in hope for what has become my favourite part of the job.

It is a job I can thank my parents for. They spotted my early potential but also provided me with such good genes; another taboo, since modern thinking has it that we are all born equal and the same. My dad was a physicist and lectured at UCL. My mother qualified as a chartered accountant but never practiced. I was their only child and had plenty of attention and stimulation. I was home schooled by my mother until aged eleven, whereupon I breezed the eleven plus examination and bagged a full academic scholarship to Haberdashers Aske. London's cleverest children were my classmates, but it was me setting the bar for them to take aim at. Always a maverick, I rejected the steeples of Oxford and Cambridge to stay in London, gaining a first in Medicine at Imperial, after which the double doors of the caring profession swung open for me. Mum encouraged me to look at research which I did, but only to keep her happy. I was never going to work in research. Top of my class, surgery was an option and my mum became rather taken with the idea of neuro-surgery. No doubt it would be a trump card to take to her bridge mornings with some of London's most competitive mothers.

But what clinched it for me was a summer and autumn working in a hospital in Santa Monica, California, which at the time was the unofficial breast surgery capital of the world. I arrived in the late 1980's, a time when the two industries in California of a higher value than Hollywood were orange juice and pornography. The place was awash with wannabe adult actors desperate for a competitive advantage, and surgeons who were happy to oblige. Young women from all over America made the pilgrimage to California to find fame as movie stars and, when such dreams were quashed, adult entertainment was there to soften their disappointment. Mostly, they hit the slab. It was not lost on me that the breast surgeons had the largest houses, fastest cars and the most attractive, albeit enhanced, wives. Money, not altruism, was my calling and also my failing. Oncologists get the gongs and they deserve them. Combatting cancer is a worthy use of anybody's abilities and I applaud them along with everyone else - but from my bigger house and with a nicer view.

My timing was perfect. I qualified as a general surgeon in 1993 and completed a two-year breast surgery specialism; just in time to surf a bonanza breast surgery wave right up to my metaphorical beach house. Since then, this wave has dipped and plateaued a little but I am still on its crest and riding high. Breast augmentation has probably peaked now but the new fashion for 'pert' has meant I am welcoming back my old double D clients. Breast surgery: the job that keeps on giving. What's not to love?

Sadly, both of my parents had passed before I really found my niche and made my mark. A shame because my success would have delighted them. Their wedding photo on my surgery wall serves as a constant reminder of my rather ordinary beginnings.

Bella dresses herself quickly while her assistants fuss over nothing. Her breasts stowed, it is now safe for her bodyguard to turn and face us all again. He is a massive man, his muscles bulging through his cavernous suit. Without question, his size is steroid assisted. I put him in his late thirties but I wouldn't give him ten more years if he keeps on the 'roids. His heart being the one muscle that he is not exercising, one day it will explode or simply give up. I would like to give him my card because men in America are increasingly not bothering with the gym, preferring the immediacy of surgery. Just as painful I imagine, so I guess the saying about pain and gain probably still applies.

Bella is handed her clutch bag by her assistant and I watch and wait for the tell-tale signs of a parting gift for her lowly surgeon. Gifts or tips from the world's wealthiest people are wildly exciting things to receive. Unlike a restaurant waiter who relies on such extras to make a sufficient income, my perks are less crucial, but this makes them no less exciting.

They used to be cash, but less so these days. Presents are now the order of the day. Gold is a personal favourite of mine. A little gleaming bar or a tube of coins always lifts my spirits. Most common is a present like a watch or jewellery. Cigars, lighters, pens, cases of wine, whisky, cufflinks, use of a private jet or a holiday home. To date my most unusual gift is a falcon, given to me by an Arab prince. I am sure that it is highly prized and valuable, but it is of no consequence to me. It is housed in Bahrain and although apparently it is mine, quite what I can do with it is a mystery. I have never even seen it and nor do I care to. Online I established that some birds can fetch half a million dollars, which would be exciting if I were not unable to sell it for fear of causing offence. So, what was the point in granting it to me then, you tight bastard?

Bella's assistant signs off the final paperwork and I nod appreciatively whilst trying to appear both professional and, at the same time, somehow demur and needy. This is a particular look which I can't really explain and yet I seem to have it mastered.

Out of the corner of my eye I spy my client, my senses on alert for any tell-tale signs. With Bella I only have her eyes to go on, but I am an expert at reading the signs. I am looking for a nod to one of her people. I note that Bella and her chief assistant make fleeting eye contact and my heart skips. I think it is on and I hope. Then Bella looks me in the eye briefly but says nothing. Nothing so intimate as a handshake for her surgeon as she sweeps dramatically from the room with the confidence that comes with a brand-new pair of head-turning bosoms. And she will need them because she will not be the only world beauty vying for his attention. Her bodyguard with equally large breasts follows and then her junior assistant falls in, leaving me with her chief aide.

"Madame Bella is grateful to you for the work and the skill that you have shown."

"Why, thank you, how very kind," I dip my head. "It has been my pleasure."

The assistant pauses, enjoying the moment. She is a beautiful woman herself, probably an ex-squeeze of his excellency, but now out to pasture and less carnal roles. She enjoys keeping me waiting. Her little moment of power over a brilliant and distinguished man; reducing me to a dog waiting for a treat. At this moment if she said 'sit', 'lie' and 'roll over', I would do all three. She holds out her hand, clutching a small velvet bag.

"A token of our appreciation."

I smile demurely as my hand shoots out and grabs it, probably a little too quickly, like a chameleon taking a slug off a leaf from five feet.

I stuff the little bag into my desk drawer in case she has a change of mind.

"Really, Madame Bella is too kind."

"Until next time, then," and she leaves.

Can't wait, I want to scream after her, but I don't of course.

Inside the pouch is a lady's watch. Tiny, but I am aware by now that size is not a factor to be concerned with. Until relatively recently I didn't understand the allure of the wristwatch. As a scientist, I am a practical man and time remains the same on whatever device it is viewed. But I have come to understand the majesty and beauty of a great timepiece; a marker of power and conspicuous wealth. An irony perhaps, because the more valuable the watch, the less likely it is that the owner needs to worry about the time. Most likely they don't have jobs to get to and people will wait for them anyway. I handle the watch carefully, my eye focussing and searching for an all-important brand. Most likely you will be familiar with Rolex, Cartier and Omega. Piaget and Chopard perhaps, but what about Du Maurier, Blancpain or Louis Erard? I could go on. There are so many brands that people pay unseemly amounts of money for and all power to them – especially so when they get bored and pass them on to me.

I study this little beauty. An Audemars Piguet in either

white gold, or hopefully platinum. Not stainless steel, surely? A high-class problem if ever there is one and I smile broadly.

CHAPTER FOUR

At that time, I did not have an inkling of what was in store for me; that Bella's gift would expose me as a man who had been lying to himself. That I had maladies and that I was not the rich, successful and happy plastic surgeon. This realisation came looking for me and punched me hard on the nose. Is this evidence for the case that I had been chosen, perhaps? Unbeknownst to me then, it was a gift that would literally save my life. This is another lofty claim but, as you are about to discover, it is the truth.

A watershed from an old life that I feel so detached from now as I write this book. It might come as a great relief to many of my readers but a new Gabriel Webber is about to emerge.

*

I put my little pouch inside my breast jacket pocket and quickly consult my itinerary. My flight for Dubai isn't leaving until 8pm so I have plenty of time to get across to my man, Maurice Cohen, in the Burlington Arcade with my new little timepiece. Maurice's family have been jewellers going back four generations; in Berlin originally and then in London since fleeing Germany. Maurice is not an easy man to like. Deeply religious, he has a superior and sanctimonious air and he is dismissive of anyone without a God - like me. He is terse too and doesn't try to conceal his disapproval of me, despite the considerable amounts of money I have generated for him. But he serves a purpose. It is his knowledge I need, not his friendship. As I have explained, I have few friends, but I am happy enough without them. I am content in my own skin and my success and my wealth are my great comforters. There are people I play bridge with, but they are just acquaintances and mostly the husbands of Judy's friends. Nice enough people, but in the main, deadly dull.

I start to hurry now, excited to get to Maurice's shop. He knows his watches as well as anyone in London and he is my go-to man to convert my gifts into cash. I have two bank accounts in Zurich, which is appropriate given that the watches I am gifted all hail from Switzerland. And there is nothing wrong in having a diverse portfolio and including money off-shore. No laws broken so long as the money is declared and known to the authorities. That said, mine is not declared and this will be an issue whenever I choose to repatriate my funds; an issue that leaves me cold and I have been avoiding for a few years now.

Maurice also advised me on my security deposit box, a recommendation which, given the infamous robbery of the Hatton Garden boxes in 2014, was invaluable. Like most people I first heard about the robbery on the radio when the details were only vague. I was driving down the Euston Road listening to Classic FM when a news bulletin came on. All I heard were the words 'daring raid' and 'London security boxes' and, for a moment, my entire world fell apart. My vision clouded and I almost drove straight into the queue for Madame Tussauds. No doubt ordinary Londoners were gleeful at the bulletin. Some good financial news for a change, with rich people having their uninsured and untaxed wealth filched. But I couldn't join in with their celebrations though, not until I knew that my booty was safe. Which it was and all thanks to

Maurice Cohen, which is still due. I had meant to thank him. I even thought about buying him a gift only I didn't get around to it and the moment just seemed to pass. My gain then. And isn't it the thought that counts?

I gather my belongings into my neat, leather carry bag when Deborah, my long-standing medical secretary, pops her head round my door.

"All set?"

"Yep, almost."

"Good". She lets the word hang a little, giving me space to elaborate. I chose to ignore this and she smiles knowingly.

"And how was Bella?" she asks.

"Oh, yes, good. You know?" I reply vaguely, conscious of what she is really enquiring about. I made the mistake of telling Deborah about my perquisites a few years back; something I regretted immediately and ever since. Unsurprisingly, Deborah is partial to gifts herself and would like her share in our spoils, which rather takes a shine off them for me.

Deborah has been with me since the very beginning of my private surgery and has done very nicely from the arrangement. Twice married, she has recently received her second set of free breast implants (although I did charge her costs this time). Occasionally I do pass on the odd gift to her but only when they are size and value appropriate. This does not apply to the (hopefully platinum) watch, currently burning a warm hole in my jacket pocket.

"Did she leave us anything?" Deborah asks cheekily. I grin at her use of the plural.

"Not for us I'm afraid. Not this time."

Deborah smiles ruefully. Tight old git.

"Passport?" she adds, a little ritual we have developed since I arrived one day at Heathrow without the blessed document. I missed my flight and almost lost a very important client in the process. Esteemed though I am, I am mindful of where I sit in life's great hierarchy and that there are certain clients who expect me to commute to them, and no problem. Have scalpel, will travel and often, in private jets and always first class, thank you very much.

The Middle East is the region that is most bountiful for me. It is a region with levels of extravagance rarely seen before and as such, it is a wonderful hunting ground for me. For all the treasures it bestows on me, I feel like Aladdin as I enjoy my highly lucrative visits. Frequently, I work in my clients' personal hospitals which are permanently staffed in case of an emergency. Some have a full cardiac surgery team on permanent stand-by and I've even heard of live organ donors housed in suites nearby, sending their pay cheques back to the sub-Continent and praying that the phone doesn't ring requiring the odd kidney or even worse, their heart. But for other less critical procedures, like cosmetic breast surgery, some restraint and planning are displayed and they send for their preferred surgeon.

"Your car is booked for 5pm. Picking you up from home?"

"Yes, that's fine. Thanks, Deborah. Emirates?"

Deborah nods. My preferred airline.

"Good, very good. And back when, Sunday evening?"

"Correct. You had a new consultation on Monday at 10am but I've managed to move it to the same time on Tuesday, just ahead of your surgery at midday.'

I smile broadly. A day off then and perhaps a visit to my security box.

"Great stuff, Deborah, thank you."

I put on my hat and smile.

"I hope Maurice has good news for you," she adds cheekily.

I laugh loudly and make a mental note to get her a little thank you gift. Something from duty free. A perfume perhaps?

I skip down the black and white tiled steps outside my office building on Hinde Street, a stunning Georgian mansion which, along with my home in Marylebone village, is the bedrock of my wealth. My office is literally a treasure trove, generating an extraordinary income from the three-other private medical practices renting floors from me. Below is a small basement residence, the income from which alone covers the building's entire fixed outgoings. The building is more lucrative than my own medical practice. I purchased it for £3 million over a decade ago. It seemed like a King's Ransom at the time, but fortune favours the brave because it has quadrupled in value and I have long dispatched the mortgage. A jewel of a building with an alluring W1 postcode, complete with a mesmerizing blue plaque declaring it to have been the residence of the famous architect, Sir Ridley James. I don't know his work but I approve of his taste in houses and I hope that, in good time, I might join him with a plaque of my own.

It is a warm spring day in London with blossom stubbornly clinging to a few trees that line my street. A few minutes' walk and I cross Wigmore Street, heading for Oxford Street and London's famous West End. Young professionals are darting about the place, juggling their salads lunches and expensive coffees with their all-important smart phones. Self-obsession and the need to be connected: another of the great paradoxes of our modern world.

Not long and I am upon the back of Selfridges, one of the world's most grand and confident department stores. Less showy and garish than Harrods, it stands proudly as the flagship store on Europe's biggest shopping street. A shop for the rich and aspirational. A building brimming with luxury goods that ordinary people can look at but can't afford. I push through the heavy doors and enjoy the instant blast of cool air from the shop's air conditioning before my senses are assaulted by the perfumes, creams and vapours of the ground floor. Sales assistants caked with make-up and dangerously long eyelashes are at the ready with their testers. Experienced as they are, they know which patrons are decent prospects and which are not. I pass by untroubled. Not even a glance from the male assistants who look both ridiculous and wonderful with their shaped eyebrows and pinched cheeks; one hand in the air with the tester and the other pressed to the back of their hip. Lips pursed and eyes wide in their wonderful gayness competition with one another.

I like gay men. They seem happy to me, I almost envy them and it is no surprise why 'camp' is so enjoyed by all. Larry

Grayson, Russell Harty, Julian Clarey, Danny La Rue, Graham Norton, Alan Carr, Alan Cumming… the list goes on and gay kitsch is fully embraced and celebrated by Selfridges, my favourite shop. It appeals to my vanity and to my ego because I can afford anything they stock and yet I make few purchases. Marks and Spencer are just across the road and I defy anyone to explain the merits of the designer suit. The only Selfridges luxury I allow myself is a salt beef sandwich from their glorious food hall. Granted, not good for my health, but too good to pass up on. A man's gotta live.

On my way to see Maurice I always pop into Selfridges; to reward myself with a sandwich but also to wander through the jewellery department and, specifically today, through their extensive and reassuringly expensive watch collection. It always cheers me, but particularly so when I have something to value. Maurice will provide a definitive secondary market value but I always like to have a figure in mind. Probably because I don't really trust him. He's too clutching to trust and I should know.

I decide that I will get to Maurice's first and then return for my unhealthy fill of salty protein. I enter the Selfridges world of luxury watches: where British shoppers gawp and the patrons from the Middle East do most of the buying.

Briskly, I pass famous marques. Today I am only interested in Audemars Piguet, or AP to those in the know. One of Switzerland's finest watchmakers if their website is to be believed. I press my inner arm against my breast jacket pocket and enjoy the reassuring feeling of the tiny pouch. I hope it is platinum which will make up for the rather disappointing leather strap.

I scan the glass display cases, my eyes squinting a little with the bright lights but mostly with my excitement.

"Can I help you sir?" an assistant asks hopefully, no doubt on commission. He has a Slavic look and a faint accent. Polish, Slovakian?

I shake my head. Sorry pal. Just looking.

I spy a watch that is similar.

"That one there…" I point through the thick glass. "Is that

watch white gold or platinum?" He barely glances.

"White gold, sir." His voice is flat now. Perhaps he has recognised me and knows my game? And so, what?

"None of these watches are platinum," the assistant adds a little pointedly, as though this is something any serious AP customer would know.

"Thank you," I mutter as I bend down to spy the price properly; not so easy with old eyes and so many numerals. I make a mental note of the number as my adrenal gland dumps a dollop of its finest into my bloodstream. Thank you, Princess Bella. You truly are a beautiful woman. I make a mental note to write her a polite letter; to enquire about her well-being and also to thank her. Not too soon though, I am ever mindful not to appear grasping. In a week or so. All in the timing, as the saying goes. I congratulate myself on my little pun as I feel once again for the tiny watch in my jacket pocket.

CHAPTER FIVE

Just as I am about to exit the store I give way to three ladies. They sweep through double doors being held open for them by a man in a dark suit. Another man, similarly dressed and complete with earpiece, follows closely behind the trio. No doubt a large black Mercedes or Rolls Royce is now parked up somewhere close, its chauffeur watching the dashboard TV with his phone on. The women are all draped in black with full face veils; their Channel glasses and bright red lipstick their only concession to the west. But beneath the austere cloaks are the most preened women who have ever lived. Everything about them is designer; their clothes, jewellery, vaginas, breasts and all facial features. My colleague Gerald Baum in California is a leading labial surgeon, currently doing a brisk trade by heading north to the new territory of designer naval surgery. These ladies are the Selfridges cash cows and mine too, God bless them. They can drop a million pounds in the blink of an eye, which is no small feat given that their false eyelashes look like draft excluders.

I skirt Grosvenor Square on into Mayfair and along to Cork Street with its art galleries. As lovely a fifteen-minute walk as I can imagine, and especially so on such a warm day with my prize in hand. The Burlington Arcade is a covered shopping precinct that has stood for nearly two hundred years, providing boutique shopping for people with excessive money and time.

Excited now, I ring the bell on Maurice's shop and wait for one of his staff to allow me entry. A young man who I do not recognise opens the door. He has a knowing look about him, as though Maurice might have talked about me. This might be paranoia but I do usually have a good instinct for such things. Immediately I don't like him and it seems to be mutual.

"Hello. I'm Gabriel Webber," I announce proudly. If my name rings any bells then he does well to disguise it.

"I'm a friend of Maurice. Is he around?"

He pauses a moment, perhaps surprised by my use of the word 'friend' or my silly question - Maurice is always around. This is his shop. Where else would he be? The assistant pushes a button under the counter.

"Maurice will be with you shortly." He disappears behind his curtain, leaving me alone.

I check my watch again, a gold Cartier that I bought from this very shop almost five years ago. It is only 1.15pm so I have plenty of time before my flight. Bella's watch will spend the weekend in my safe at home and then on Monday I will transfer it to my security box. I could do it today but these things shouldn't be rushed. Visiting my security box has become my greatest pleasure and something to savour. Other men play golf, go to galleries, the theatre and dinner. I visit my jewels. My weekend ahead will be a financial bonanza and I have my Monday visit to look forward to. Life is good.

I look around his old and pristine shop, mindful that the squat and scruffy owner will emerge at any moment. I note the camera in the corner, reminding me that I am not alone. I expect that Maurice is watching me now from his office while he stuffs his face. It makes me a little self-conscious as I peer through the display cabinets at the treasures within. The cabinets themselves are works of art. Oaked framed, with highly polished timber securing the curved and delicate glass. But it is the jewels within which really captivate. Rows and rows of watches, mainly female timepieces in gold and platinum, some crusted with diamonds and rubies. All formerly owned by the elite and no doubt each with extraordinary tales of how they ended up on sale again: bankruptcy, divorce, probate, theft, adultery and much else besides. There is no Audemars Piguet I note as I wonder where the hell Maurice might be and why he is keeping me waiting? How rude of him.

His face will fall when I explain that Bella's watch will be joining my collection and is not for him to sell on. I just need its value, which is a little awkward. I could go online but this is never very satisfactory as figures vary wildly. Maurice, however, has his podgy finger on the pulse and it is his figure that I will plug into my spread sheet.

I look at my watch again. A further ten minutes have passed and now I am bloody angry. So unnecessary and most unlike the ever-punctual Maurice Cohen. I have a good mind to go and find him. But I don't of course. I am too refined and so my anger continues to stir. I am looking directly into his security camera now, and with my most displeased look in-order to hurry him along. He remains a no-show.

There is much about Maurice that I admire. His devotion to his family and his love for his God in the face of growing anti-Semitism. Down through the ages, when caricaturists have intended to hurt and offend, it is the face of Maurice that they draw. Maurice is small, fat and balding with a flaky scalp that doesn't seem to bother him very much. He has alert but shifty eyes and pendulous jowls which sit around a mouth that seems to never fully close. With his kippah, black suit, white shirt and black hat, Maurice proudly and fiercely embraces his Judaism. Good for him. The Jewish people are remarkable and it is their success and the politics of envy at the heart of any scorn they endure.

And finally, the man himself appears. Maurice breezes into his shop and right enough, he has a mouth full of food - a good portion of which is stuck in his unkempt beard. I glare at him and then my watch as I wait for an apology which doesn't arrive. He hardly looks at me and grunts the barest hello. Immediately, I sense that something is askew but I can't discern what it is.

"I've been waiting almost fifteen minutes," I begin, but Maurice only shrugs, silencing me. He fixes me with a cold, unsettling stare.

"Well, you've had plenty of time then?" He says loftily.

"What do mean?" I ask.

He gestures to his wares and then refocuses on me. "Seen anything you like?"

This wrong foots me and I look at him oddly.

"Anything you want to buy?" He adds pointedly.

"Er…"

I feel Bella's watch in my pocket but I hesitate.

"Because this is a shop, you know? It's what I do. I sell things."

I don't appreciate his patronising tone and this is not the opening I had been expecting. Maurice's face becomes harder and I need to gather myself and try to adjust. He has an air to him, as though he knows my game and that he is no longer willing to play along.

In the last few years my new found love of hoarding has cost Maurice dearly. I used to want cash (and this suited him perfectly), but quickly cash lost its allure. Too difficult to spend, cumbersome to store and frankly, boring to look at and flick through. But once my eyes were opened to the glint of jewellery, it quickly gripped me. Don't misunderstand me, I still delight in logging into my various investment accounts for a bit of balance porn, but it pales against the thrill of owning real treasure. A gold ingot is so much more seductive than digits and zeros on a computer screen.

And this is my great failing: my obsession with wealth. I know it now. It is an illness, a first world condition that can rot from within and be as pernicious as any mainstream disease. My success is my failing then; just another paradox of my life.

My safety deposit box is my great refuge and my very guilty pleasure. I visit regularly, at least twice a month. I allocate time and schedule it into my diary. It is a facility a little along from the recently refurbed Kings Cross Station. Housed in a non-descript building, passers-by have no idea of the treasures within. But inside the building, the luxuries and soothing wealth are all-apparent. It is warm and welcoming. It has thick carpets throughout, with complimentary drinks and freshly made canapes of all descriptions, served by suitably discreet and demur staff. I love the place. By appointment only, the viewing rooms are peaceful and assuring. Quiet, comfortable and completely private. They can be booked for up to an hour and I use the full allocation as I empty my box carefully and like to sit with my bounty all around me. I do regular audits and valuations and enjoy adjusting my neat spreadsheets as I make additions to my collection.

I like to try on the different watches, sometimes on both wrists and even up my arms. It's gaudy, but I'm afraid just the beginning of something much darker, for I discovered the fetish that men can develop over all things female.

It began with the attractive female staff at the facility from which my imagination took hold. One young and very beautiful employee was largely to blame. She was foreign, probably Czech or even Russian, early thirties and achingly lithe and attractive. I would imagine us together in my viewing room with my jewellery all around us.

Unfortunately, this coincided with a visit to our home of Judy's niece from Israel. Pretty enough, but with a supple and gymnastic figure, she barely stayed a week but I was not prepared for the impact this would have on me. Particularly so the pair of knickers that she left behind in our tumble dryer. Easily done given the tiny size of the garment. I had never thought of myself as a pervert but I was helpless to resist and quickly found myself upstairs, wearing only her garment and masturbating furiously. A remarkable awakening, since my libido had all but died. I had never even viewed pornography, but suddenly I faced a new dawn and a slippery slope. I started making furtive visits to Soho lingerie shops to purchase garments that I would bring with me on visits to my security box. And there, dressed in my best lace smalls, draped in jewellery, I would have the most elaborate and expensive wanks on earth.

"Well?" Maurice snaps, as though it is him being kept waiting and that his time is pressing. I look at him curiously.

"I haven't got all day," he spits and I am astounded.

"Well I must say, Maurice, your tone-"

"Never you mind, my bloody tone. Do you understand?"

I stare at the man, unsettled by his aggression and suddenly unsure of myself. "So, you want to buy something, or don't you?"

Ah, so my suspicions about my lack of purchases appear to be correct; not that I am prepared or indeed, know how to respond. I just stand still, floundering and as he waits, his bulbous tongue roots into his beard for errant crumbs.

"Or have you come for just another free valuation?"

My eyes narrow at this awkward question and his hand strengthens even more. A valuation is not going to feed his kids. At the last count he had five children, all boys. A ridiculous number and completely irresponsible. God-damn religions, really?

"Well…" I begin softly, trying to dial things down a notch or two. But I falter. Because what I do with Bella's watch is my business and my business alone, especially since it might involve dangling it over my satin knickers as they struggle to contain my hungry and erect penis. But I can't say this of course.

"Your Patek." Maurice barks matter-of-factly.

Instantly this strikes a nerve and I am alarmed. This is not a question, but feels more like a threat.

"Yes, what about it?" I ask fearfully.

"Let me sell it for you."

I am aghast, practically winded.

"What?"

"Get you eighteen for it, by Monday…"

I can't respond and just shake my head in disbelief. I am not selling my Patek.

"In your account by Tuesday so you can go online and gawp at your money."

This stops me again and Maurice senses his victory. I need a moment to steady myself.

"Well?"

"But that's my favourite watch."

Maurice tuts. "Is it?"

"Yes."

"Then why don't you wear it?"

"How dare you! How the hell would you know if I wear it or not?" I shoot back, trying to get on the front foot. But Maurice is not threatened. He just smirks and doesn't bother to answer. He knows I don't wear it. He has a new-found confidence about him which is unnerving. What the hell is going on? I am the eminent surgeon here, not to mention the bloody customer. Isn't the customer, always right? I decide to change tack and take a more superior line. I force myself to smile.

"Right, well, I'm not quite sure what exactly is going on here,' I begin slowly, 'but what I do with my Patek is frankly none of your business. I love that watch."

"Oh, is that right?"

"Yes. It is."

"Good for you. And I love my kids. Not that you would understand. You don't love anyone," he spits venomously. I try to smile and appear assured but this is not easy. He's wheeled out his ugly kids in our exchanges before but not with such spite and I am shocked and shaken.

"If you're not going to buy something then I would like you to leave."

My mouth falls at this. Am I being thrown out of his shop?

"Oh, really? Is that right?" I barely manage.

"Yes, that's right. And don't bother me again."

"What?"

"Don't come back, unless you've fetched that Patek out of your sad little cave."

My eyes widen now in alarm, verging on panic. This comment is so barbed and loaded that he might have poked me in the eye. His calling it my 'cave' as such is particularly devastating because this is how I too affectionately refer to it. And I don't like his implication either; that I am a hoarder and a miser, even though he is dead right on both counts. Nor do I care for his use of the word 'unless', as though I need his bloody permission to do anything.

I have only one Patek Phillipe. It is the jewel in my crown and I am not about to part with it, and certainly not at the behest of Maurice bloody Cohen.

The famous brand of watch, Patek Phillipe, is relevant here because of the smug way that they peddle their clobber. They advertise in upmarket magazines with the lofty boast that their watches are not owned, but merely kept for successive generations, and feature unfeasibly suave and handsome fathers and sons. If ever an advert were designed to rankle with me and expose the great issue that plagued me; what to do with and how to dispose of my wealth.

We will all pass and none of us can take anything with us; a bitter reality that every Pharaoh discovered the hard way. This is my nemesis and I feel nauseous thinking about it. Not the idea of my mortality, but of leaving behind my hard-earned gains. But what is the alternative? To spend it all in time for the reaper's visit?

Last month I attended a funeral of yet another colleague. A surgeon who seemingly had it all and yet the poor wretch didn't see his sixtieth birthday. I have some distant cousins in America but I don't know them and have no intention of brightening up their world when I part. An insoluble problem then which becomes more acute with each passing birthday and every new ache and pain. Imponderable and pathetic because I obsess with acquiring more wealth and then fret that I won't have time to spend it. It is no way to live and yet I cannot change. My whole life is a hopeless contradiction. Liquidating my assets is the most logical solution but what to spend it on? Another house, a castle somewhere, a plane, a boat… More and better food? But doesn't appetite wane with age anyway?

My mind wandering to such matters seems to be the final

straw for Maurice as he waves a hand in the air and makes to return to his office.

"Where are you going?" I plead pathetically.

"Back to work, where do you think?"

"But-"

"I have a shop to pay for."

"Yes, I can see that but-"

"Can you? Only I'm not blinking Selfridges!"

This stops me again. Damn him. Always a step ahead. I eye him carefully, wondering if he knows of my little ritual. His earlier 'cave' reference was surely just a pot shot, but his Selfridges slight is more oblique and it makes me wonder… He might well have seen me browsing in the department store or more likely, have had a report back.

"And is this how you speak to all your customers?" I ask lamely, rather teeing him up.

""No, you old fool," he barks. "Because you're not a customer."

Bastard. Another excellent point and I reel again.

"And you don't think that there are other jewellers in London?" I ask.

Maurice's air of superiority is unassailable now. He smiles as though he has been waiting for this moment, and he turns side on so he can put his shoulder into delivering his rebuke.

"Yes, Bond Street is full of them. But they'll want paying. People need to eat."

"Oh, really…"" I begin to parry. "Meaning, what exactly?" I ask, immediately cross with myself because of how utterly pathetic it is of me. What the hell is wrong with me? But my defences are breached now and I am overwhelmed. Maurice shakes his head slowly and exhales, as though tired of my presence.

"Gabriel, do you know something?"

"What?" I ask. I might as well have stuck my chin out for him.

"You really are pathetic."

I hear him, but I cannot respond.

"As stupid as you are, however did you become a doctor?"

I blink furiously. I have been called lots of things in my life but never stupid. Unfortunately, Maurice isn't finished yet.

"You come in here, waving your stinking rich willy about and you expect me to admire it?"

Boom. Another punch to my midriff.

"How vulgar-"

Maurice chuckles and points to himself.

"Me, vulgar?" I barely manage.

"Yes."

Maurice now points at my face. "When did you last pray?"

"Er…"

"Pray to God. Said thank you?"

"Er, I don't. I'm not…"

"Okay then. When did you last do something for someone else?"

My mind scrambles now. I need an answer but nothing occurs. Nothing at all. Maurice flashes a knowing smile.

"Nothing, no? Anything for anyone. When were you last kind? Or generous? And I don't mean stapling a pair of plastic tits to a rich bitch."

"How dare you."

This is a pathetic retort, I know, but the best I can do.

"No, Gabriel. How dare you? Hoarding women's jewellery... getting off on it too, I shouldn't imagine. And you call me vulgar?"

Jesus Christ. The Cave. The Patek and now my wanking which he can't possibly know about. But all direct hits. I am dizzy now and the room is spinning.

"You horrible little man," I barely manage. "I am a-"

"A doctor, I know. God help us all."

'Maurice, please…'

"Do you know what?" Maurice fixes me with his glare. "You're like a Dickensian character."

I can't speak now; my mouth is too dry and my lungs have all but collapsed. My gloves are down, my chin exposed. It is just a matter of time.

"Like a modern Fagin."

I shake my head and continue to gasp for air like a carp on a riverbank.

"Do you know what we call you?" Maurice continues, now with a wicked glint in his eye. I stare back at him and then shake my head, although masochistically. I need to know.

"A squirrel. We call you The Squirrel."

And with this, metaphorically, I slump onto the canvass. Softened by his heavy shots, I am finally floored by 'squirrel'.

I glare back at my nemesis. Squirrel? Did I hear him correctly?

"Meaning, what exactly?" I ask, like a puppet on his string. Maybe he's right and I am bloody stupid. Maurice the puppet master is succinct and devastating. And his delivery is brilliant, as though he had it planned all along. I see his theatrical side for the first time, screwing his face up and aping the hand movements of the arboreal tailed rat.

"Busy, busy, busy, Gabriel the squirrel, gathering his nuts and burying them. More and more nuts. More than he will ever need. A lonely little man, lost in greed and love of himself, because he has no one else to share his nuts with…"

"Stop it," I plead.

"What do you do with it all, sit there and gawp at it? Is that it?'

"Stop it. Why are you doing this to me?"

"I don't know. Because it feels right."

"Well, it's not. It's bloody cruel. And it's not right."

"No. You're wrong. My wife's cancer wasn't right. This is."

"But she survived."

Maurice glares at me and I whimper.

"Please, why are you doing this to me?" I repeat.

"You keep telling me how clever you are. So, figure things out for yourself and then come here and explain yourself. Until then, get out of my shop."

With this, Maurice pivots on the worn heels of his cheap shoes and vanishes through the beaded curtains. I couldn't have responded, even if he'd given me the chance. Right on cue, his assistant reappears and it is obvious that he has seen the whole exchange. At least he has the grace to look embarrassed for me, and even a little sad. I need to leave. The assistant gestures to the exit and I nod. We approach the ornate door together. Leaving the shop is my priority. He barely opens the catch and I am through the gap immediately. Jettisoned from the shop, like a cowboy hitting the dirt with the saloon doors swinging behind him. My character shredded, my dignity in pieces.

I pull my hand through my hair and try to make sense of what has just happened. I have been assaulted. I am a victim of a hate crime. I could probably have him locked up for something or other, surely?

I stagger away from the shop, conscious of being leered at by Maurice in his upstairs office; thrilled at vanquishing me. He exposed my failings so completely, dare I say it - surgically. I emerge from the arcade, into the piercing sunshine. I need to steady myself and catch my breath. The beautiful day provides no warmth or comfort. I have been traduced and I am desolate.

I look up at the sky, the plume of a jet the only blemish in the bright blue. It is where I will be shortly, in my first-class seat, but it offers me no solace. It appals me and I feel ashamed. A day that had been going so well has now become a nightmare.

Allow me to use the third person to mark the gravity of the situation: Gabriel Webber is wounded, perhaps even fatally, and he is bloody terrified.

CHAPTER SIX

I have never felt such rage and a sense of injustice in my entire life. The bile that is hurled at me online is nothing to the hurt and anger that Maurice has just inflicted on me in person.

My mind continues to race; poring over every foul utterance which came from his fetid mouth. Of all the people to lay me so low. My heart pounds, making me dizzy and lightheaded. Damn, I should have eaten earlier. Perhaps then I could have returned fire and put the fat bastard on his arse? Too late now. I am in fight or flight mode but have done neither, rooted to the spot as surplus adrenalin wreaks havoc with my body.

I take some deep breaths, always overrated in my opinion, as I continue to search for some understanding. I run over each insult in my mind as best I can remember as a form of self-harm: old, grasping, lonely, stupid, hoarding, vulgar and finally, squirrel-like. I see his ugly little face and I freeze frame as I recall his jibes.

'You don't have anyone.'

He is right of course. I don't have anyone. And instantly on this warm day, I feel ice cold.

I pull my hands through my hair. I have plenty of people, I assure myself. Judy, my wife, who I will not be able to share this indignity with since she knows nothing of my hidden wealth… and then the moniker, squirrel, hits me hard again.

I shake my head and sniff to clear my nose. And so, what, I tell myself. Being called a squirrel is comical and pathetic. There are worse animals to be compared to: a cockroach, pig, skunk, snake, shark. I'll take squirrel any day. Why then am I so hurt? Who would imagine that 'squirrel' could ever trump 'Nazi?'

And then something occurs. I stop walking and my mood dips even further. Again, I replay the confrontation with my tormenter and I pause on a single word: 'we'. I run it through again, just to be sure. I visualise him; his bulbous, ugly mouth. He definitely used the plural.

'Do you know what we call you?'

Which means that people are talking about me. But which people, and what are they saying?

I imagine people at Maurice's synagogue sitting around and hearing about the greedy squirrel of a surgeon, making his filthy money from 'fake tits'. Certainly, Maurice has a crude side and a way with language. I imagine people cackling at the expense of the grasping surgeon. Sanctimonious bastards.

Bringing up his wife's cancer again was a low blow and unnecessary. I scold myself because I should have explained that I do corrective surgery on post-operative breast cancer patients. Alas, the beauty of hindsight. I even consider returning to share this little nugget with him but I decide against it, mainly because I can predict his repost.

'And this corrective surgery? For the NHS is it? Or is it private? Making money out of death and misery then?'

Most likely he wouldn't even open the shop for me and leave me hanging outside; a humiliation I could not possibly bear. God, how I hate him.

I stumble onto Bond Street without really thinking about where I am heading. I try to reassure myself with more unfavourable animals: the weasel, fox, hyena, cuckoo, vulture… but none of them help. But they pale against Maurice's squirrel. The word repeats in my head on a loop, punctuated with memories of further insults hurled at me.

'…sit there and gawp at it?'

A shaft of panic now grips me. Maurice knows the location of my 'cave'. But worse: has someone at the facility compromised me? Just how private is the viewing room, I ask myself. Perhaps it is monitored for security and insurance purposes? My eyes widen at such a wretched thought. Jesus Christ! If my masturbatory habits are ever exposed? My career, marriage, everything will be over! I clutch at my chest in pain. It will solve my legacy conundrum however, because I will happily clamber over waterloo bridge to my watery end. At this very moment, a bus passes-by and a macabre thought occurs… but it is moving too slowly and would probably only paralyse me anyway.

At this moment, I hate Maurice Cohen more than anything I have ever hated. How dare he say such ugly and accurate things. I try to laugh it off. A squirrel for pity's sake? But my hurt continues. I am ravenous and lightheaded. Unstable on my feet, I might even faint.

I lean against a post box. I must get some food and something for my thirst. This feeling will pass. I am a surgeon. Damn it, I am Gabriel Webber. What I really need is to offload and share. But who? Not Judy. 'What bloody security box?' she will want to know. Not Deborah either for the same reason. Then who? There really is no one, and I am reminded of Maurice again and his cruel tongue.

As an aside, I cannot adequately explain my secrecy. Hiding my treasure - it is not a contingency fund in the way that some duplicitous men require; their getaway stash for the exit with their mistress. I don't have a mistress and never have had. It is just my stuff. I like having it and, pathetic as it is, that is the only explanation I have. People are complicated and this is my foible. And so, Maurice is correct then? I am a squirrel. Greedy beyond my needs and I will never have enough.

I consider this for a moment. It is quite a moment for me and on a fitting location, one of the wealthiest shopping streets on earth. Large black cars are illegally parked, their drivers waiting patiently as their charges empty boutiques of stuff they don't need. Ahead of me to my right (and bang on cue) is the Patek Philippe store, as though to taunt me even more.

I need to get off Bond Street. It is busy with pedestrians heading in all directions. People need to give ground and accommodate each other but my timing is all wrong and frequently I bump shoulders and people tut loudly. A man in a doorway sits hunched with an empty coffee cup in front of him. He has a pathetic scrap of cardboard on which he has scrawled something that I don't wish to read. At least he has the decency to beg quietly; less intrusive and much easier to ignore. If he is homeless at all of course. A cunning opportunist perhaps, only in this doorway because the shop is being refitted and it's the workmen's lunch break. I glance at the man. He certainly has a look about him. Get a job, pal. It's why people the world over are coming here: to work.

In my haste I decide he is a professional beggar, not that begging is a real job or a profession. It is pathetic, like stealing from the mouths of the genuinely destitute. And with this I absolve myself completely of any guilt in ignoring him. This is a hollow victory since I never give money to street people anyway, even the ones who are clearly in need. There are virtuous reasons for this: that it legitimises poor life choices and exacerbates the problem; because I pay my taxes; and because isn't it the job of our bloody government to sort out such problems. More hollow arguments since the problem remains and their plight is truly awful. It is unimaginable not to have a place to live, but then, isn't everything relative? Homeless people must have community at least; a shared experience and kinship. Solidarity. Which is more than I have in my hour of need, so who is the person most unfortunate here? I have problems of my own pal. Apparently, I'm a bloody squirrel.

I quicken my step past the Patek Phillipe heir-fucking-loom store and now break into a gentle run. I must get off Bond Street and be somewhere quiet so that I can gather myself. Up ahead is a side street. I don't know the name and I don't care. I fling myself around the corner and mercifully it is quiet. I stop and lean forward as I breathe in deeply. My heart is still pounding and I momentarily wonder if I might be having a heart murmur, or even a stroke. I close my eyes and tell myself that I am fine. That my crisis will abate.

"Are you alright mate?"

Startled, I open my eyes. A young man, an office worker, is staring at me. He looks concerned and is being kindly. I nod my head as best I can but I don't thank him because I am embarrassed. He continues to stare which is a little unnerving.

"You're sure? Only you don't-"

"Yes, yes, I'm fine. I'm fine," I snap. What I would give to sit down with him and unload? But where would I begin? And there in a nutshell is the hopelessness of my life.

I get on my way again. Ahead, in another doorway, I notice another crouched figure and I sigh. Fucking beggars, really? I should cross the road to avoid an encounter. Begging is a numbers game, which is the reason they select busy places to loiter. Peculiar then that this loser would choose such a quiet street to wait. Their lunch hour perhaps, some down time. Or, more likely, he's scored and is zoned out. I note the absence of the empty cup which means I'm more likely to be petitioned. Such pleas always aggrieve me. Such an intrusion, only made worse when they call out a virtuous but snide and loaded, 'thanks anyway' and 'have a nice day'.

How does anyone end up so utterly hopeless anyway? To exist without anyone in the world and so pathetically that they have to rely on total strangers. They must have families? Parents at least and if they've died, then siblings, cousins, uncles… And if not family, then friends? Someone with a roof and a floor.

But, whatever their circumstances, they are not my fault. I have not caused their misery. Approaching the beggar and feeling as vulnerable as I do, I should probably cross the road, but I don't. I immediately realise this is a mistake but it is too late to feign a phone call; my preferred strategy when confronted by the ghastly bibbed collectors who fan across the pavement like a blasted drag net.

I am level with the wretch now, keeping my eyes forward. I wait for the plea but nothing comes. I am relieved and grateful. Perhaps, somehow, he knows that I have been assaulted and mugged already this morning. But then my luck runs out. I am a few paces past when a furtive plea breaks the silence, as though he has just woken up and decides to try his luck. Nothing ventured…

"Excuse me, sir?"

The words startle me. Firstly, because of the use of the word 'sir', and that it doesn't feel saccharine and cynical. Then, that the person is English and even well-spoken. But mostly because it is not a man at all, but a woman.

I am annoyed too at being so caught because what she can possibly want with me apart from the blinking obvious? All my instincts tell me to ignore her and to continue on. I owe her nothing and she has no right to make me feel awkward. Plus, I am past her already and in the laws of begging, this means that I am allowed to move on. Aren't these the rules? And yet I find myself stopping and turning around to see that she has a further surprise for me: she is young. Early thirties is my best guess but she could be younger, prematurely aged by the street. We make eye contact and consider each other for a moment as we dance around the inevitable: her need for money and my reasons why I have none to give.

"Have you the time, please?" she asks and completely wrong foots me, not for the first time today. First, Maurice bloody Cohen and now a bloody beggar. She has an air about her, and it is not just her manners. Her wording is peculiar. Have you the time? Vague and non-specific. The time? The time for what, I wonder. I have a plane to catch. Nonetheless, her question is welcome because I am no longer thinking about Maurice bloody Cohen. I look at my expensive watch.

"Just before 2."

"Okay… thank you." She smiles and I wait for her next question, but she adds nothing. I can see now that she isn't a bad looking woman. She might even be rather beautiful. She has boyish good looks in the style of Audrey Hepburn. Bernard Shaw's Pygmalion is playing out before me.

"Is that it then?" I snap, offering her an opportunity to get to the bloody point. But she shrugs and looks at me quizzically.

"What do you mean?" she asks.

"Well, is that all you want? The time?"

She shrugs again.

"Well, that depends."

In my state of anxiety, this is all a little oblique and I feel my patience thinning.

"On what?"

"I don't know. What's on offer, I suppose?"

I sneer at her guile and I wonder if there isn't a lewd insinuation to our encounter. Her eyes flicker and I reason that she might in fact be fully employed in the oldest profession of all.

"I don't have any money if that's what you're implying."

This is not true of course. I have pots of the stuff, more than I can ever spend, but what I mean is: I don't have any money that I consider to be spare. And certainly not on me at this very moment.

I rarely use cash nowadays and carry it only as a contingency. In my wallet I always have four brand new fifty-pound notes and, on the rare occasion that I break into one, I replace the smaller denominations with a brand new fifty. It is just neater. I keep a huge jar of discarded cash in my garage and a neat stack of brand-new fifties in my home safe. I do, therefore, have money on my person but not in a denomination that I am prepared to part with, no matter how pretty and intriguing she is.

"Why do you need the time?" I ask, aware that this might appear rude. Presumably she doesn't have a flight to catch? She thinks for a moment and then shrugs casually.

"Just because, you know…"

No, I don't know.

"…perhaps time is the one thing that we all share?"

It is an unusual answer, philosophical almost, and in

keeping with my unusual day. She has an air about her which is unsettling.

"Because we all get the same time, right?" she adds with another smile.

Reluctantly, I nod.

"Oh, and air? Or oxygen? And sunshine as well, I guess." she adds and I grow wearier still.

"And rain?" I suggest but she disagrees, scrunching her nose and shaking her head.

"What do you mean?" I ask.

"Well, some people can avoid the rain. They have umbrellas. Coats. Houses.'

It's a good point, well-made, and I nod. Powerful stuff. Very worthy. One of the big issues of modern life but I really need to get on. I have a crisis of my own to manage.

"And maybe not time either?" She rethinks.

My eyes narrow.

"Because you look very busy, so maybe time is something that I have more of than you? You look like a man in a hurry."

"I am. I have a plane to catch."

She nods easily. "Right, well, there we are. I don't. So, I have more time than you."

She makes this sound attractive, as though she is the lucky one in our equation.

"So please, don't let me keep you," she says. Her assuredness is unsettling, as though she is dismissing me. And still she has not asked for money.

"Where are you going? Anywhere nice?"

I shrug. "Dubai."

"Okay, nice. Not been but it's on my list."

It is a most peculiar exchange. Almost beguiling given the circumstances but most welcome as a distraction from my earlier assault. I think of Cohen and his barbs. Would he recognise me as a squirrel if he could see me now, engaging with a homeless person? In this moment, I am resolved to giving her some money. One in the eye for Cohen. But certainly not a fifty-pound note. I start to make some calculations. I assume she can't change a fifty herself, although, peculiar as she is, it wouldn't be such a surprise if she has card payment facilities. Do you take contactless?

During my dithering she continues to consider me, and still she doesn't ask for anything. As she alluded to, she is the one with time, not me. Beyond her and further up the street is a café, which I decide is ideal. I can buy her something to eat and then let her keep some of my change. A perfect plan. Fuck you, Cohen. Excited now and without saying anything, I hurry past her and towards the café. I catch her eye as I pass and I hope that she sees my intent.

I enter the café a little out of breath and quickly survey the stock. I am slightly agitated because I imagine I have disappointed her by running off without a word and so I need to be quick. I realise I am excited at the prospect of seeing her face when I reappear.

There is a customer ahead of me but the lady serving can feel my presence and urgency. I spy what is on offer in the glass cabinet. A large beef sandwich looks appetising enough but I wonder about her eating habits. So many youngsters these days are off meat, and she does have the look of a Brighton vegan about her. Not that she is in any position to be choosey.

Soon I am being served and I order a large coffee and an old-style iced bun, much like the cakes that I used to enjoy as a child.

"Flat white? Americano, Latte, Cappuccino…"

What a nonsense when it's all the bloody same thing. My guess is that the lady serving is Polish and yet she doesn't appear to be very excited about being in the world's most vibrant city (if guide books are to be believed).

"Yes, whatever. Latte is fine." I worry again about veganism and the fads of the youth. The lady gets to work on the coffee and I shuffle from foot to foot. She puts the coffee on the counter and then fishes for the tongs and the bun. Once bagged, she sees my brand new fifty-pound note and her face turns even more sour. It practically curdles as she takes my money.

"Err... in my change, could I have some tens please?"

She obliges and hastily I shove the notes in my trouser pocket before gathering my purchases. I head for the door, almost as excited as I have been all day (that moment reserved for Bella's generosity earlier on).

Outside of the shop I hold the coffee aloft, almost like an offering, but to my horror, she is gone. And with her, my excitement evaporates. I scan the street up and down and then take in the doorways, looking for a pair of knees. There is nothing. I can only have been a few minutes and yet she has vanished. And so, my anguish returns and the image of Maurice Cohen envelopes me again.

"Damn it!" I should have told her. Why didn't I tell her?

My cruel day worsens. What must she think of me? Especially given our unusual exchange and improbable connection. Or is this just something that I am imagining because I am desperate and vulnerable?

How pitiful I am. Clearly, she didn't feel anything, or else she would not have left so promptly. As she said, she doesn't have a plane to catch. And how mean spirited of me, to give her the time and nothing else when her needs were so obvious. She hadn't asked for money because she hadn't needed to. Again, I am haunted again by Maurice's insult: the squirrel with his nuts; nuts that he won't share with anyone.

I am alone again, with a sugared coffee I can't drink and a bun that I can't stomach, famished though I am. I feel hopeless.

What a loathsome individual, Maurice Cohen truly is. If I didn't have a plane to catch I might return to his shop this instant and punch him on his bloody nose.

CHAPTER SEVEN

By the time I get back to Oxford Street I am completely despondent. It is as busy as ever when my phone vibrates in my jacket pocket but with my hands full, I will struggle to answer it. I wonder if I should leave it until another vibration forces my hand and I decide to at least try. I set the coffee cup on the filthy pavement, darkened over the years by layers of detritus that I try not to think about. If I had passed a bin I would have chucked the cup and bun already, and I would leave it on the pavement now if I wasn't burdened with a sense of decency. Still vibrating, I scramble frantically now. I don't know why because it will only be Deborah or my wife; neither of whom excite me very much. A call from Maurice Cohen is what I want. Calling to apologise. I see on the screen that it is Deborah calling.

"Hello."

"Gabe, okay good. I'm glad I reached you."

"What's up?"

"There's been a change."

"Right?"

"Nothing to worry about. Your client's office in Qatar called. Something's up, their end. He didn't say what and I didn't ask."

"No."

"Now you're out on a jet, out of City at 19.40, direct to Qatar. Same client but different clinic for the consultation and then you'll fly on to Dubai for the two procedures already booked. I've charged them an extra day which they've agreed."

I shrug and check my watch. A private jet would usually lift my spirits but not today.

"Okay, fine. So, 19.40 out of City?"

"Yep, your new car pick up is 4.30pm from your house. Do I need to text you this, just so you've got it?"

Something across the street catches my eye and I stop listening.

"Gabriel?" Deborah's voice rises as she suspects a dropped call.

"Shall I text you?"

"Err…" I strain my eyes so that I can see better but a bus obscures my view. I need to move.

"Gabriel?"

"Yes, fine, text it."

I end the call and put the phone away without taking my eyes off the bus. Finally, it moves, but only to be replaced by a taxi moving from the opposite direction. My view still blocked, I try to manoeuvre; craning my neck, my eyes darting to and fro, hoping that I am correct. The coffee is important again and I fumble for it on the ground without taking my eyes from the taxi. The traffic lights change and the taxi inches forward; not enough to cheer its passenger but sufficient to clear my view. And there she is. I squint for a moment to make sure that it's her. I am certain that it is and I am thrilled. She is standing idly alongside the people distributing free copies of The Evening Standard. I dash into the road, almost calling out to her as I attempt to cross Oxford Street.

I catch her attention by the time I reach the middle of the road but I have to wait to complete my crossing. She still has that smile of hers and I hold her coffee aloft by way of an explanation. Suddenly, I feel nervous. Stupid even and, as I cross the road, I wonder what I might say.

"Sorry," I begin, "I didn't think that you'd leave so soon."

She doesn't say anything but gives me a smile which somehow makes things worse.

"You know, from where I saw you? Where we met?" It comes out as a question.

"Oh, right."

"You see, I bought you a coffee and err..." I tail off, feeling suddenly creepy, but she smiles easily enough.

"You should have said."

"Yes, I know. I thought that. I'm sorry. I was cross with myself when you'd disappeared so quickly so I'm glad I caught you."

I sound a little urgent now and probably too needy. Her smile drops.

"Right," She says.

"And a shame to waste it, right?" I hold up my offering again.

"But you could have drank it yourself?"

"Yes, there is that… but I went with sugar in your coffee. I wasn't too sure…"

She nods and smiles again.

"Yeah, good shout. I'm easy."

"Oh, good."

"Beggars can't be choosers, eh?"

"No, I guess not."

It is all highly irregular; a man chasing through London after a homeless girl. But she seems unperturbed, relaxed enough and not frightened anyway. Not that I am particularly foreboding. A small, balding, middle-aged man in a suit. But then, street people are so vulnerable. The lowest life expectancy of any social group. I suppose this means they need to be on guard – especially an attractive young woman. She doesn't seem alarmed however and happily takes my meagre offering.

"Well, this is very kind of you. Thank you."

"I just felt the urge, you know? To help."

"Good. Well, I'm glad you did. Thank you."

I nod, happy now.

"Feels good doesn't it?" she adds loftily.

"Err…"

Certainly, this is the happiest I have been all day, or since Bella's gift at least and so yes, I agree with her. It does.

"Although, I expect you'd have preferred money instead?"

She shrugs. A polite way of agreeing, perhaps?

"Any act of kindness is very welcome. No matter how small."

This is entirely new territory for me. There is something unerring about her, she has an interesting way with words and, I notice, no trace of any accent.

She sips her coffee.

"I went with two-"

She chuckles. "It's fine. I prefer sweeteners anyway."

We both laugh and I add 'sense of humour' to the mental list of her characteristics which I have discerned so far. Her green eyes hold my attention. I notice the signs of her lifestyle. Her worn clothes and dirty hands. She has blackened finger nails, one of which is missing altogether. A car door perhaps? I want to ask but I don't want to frighten her, nor to have her vanish again. It sounds ridiculous but I like her and hope that our impromptu meeting might somehow continue.

"Look, why don't you dump that?" I suggest.

"What? Why?"

"It's probably cold already."

"No, it's fine."

"Okay, fine. But-' I hesitate and look about, hardly believing what I am about to suggest and struggling for the correct words.

"Perhaps I could buy you something proper to eat? Something hot, at least."

I worry now about the connotations of this. She looks surprised but not frightened and so I dare to continue.

"We could go up the road to Selfridges. They do hot sandwiches and you can have a coffee anyway you like it."

Immediately she shakes her head. Perhaps her curiosity is

turning to suspicion and I need to exonerate myself…

"Please, there's nothing to worry about. Believe me, this is not a thing. You have nothing to fear and I don't want anything from you."

I tail off, partly because this is not strictly true. I want her company, but I can't explain this without spooking her.

"I don't normally do this." I start again.

"You don't?"

"No. This is a first for me. I usually ignore homeless people," I say, regretting it immediately.

"So, why now then? Why me?"

A fair question, one that could sound accusatory only, from her, it doesn't. She seems simply intrigued. And now it is my turn to smile because I do not have an answer for her.

"Do you know what? I don't know," I begin blandly. "Something just occurred to me. I just felt a need to help."

Her eyes narrow as she considers this.

"Well?" I ask. "How about it? Something hot to eat?"

Her eyes ponder me for a moment.

"You're not a journalist, are you?"

"No," I laugh, happy for the release. "I hate journalists."

"Or a writer of some kind?"

"No. I am definitely not a writer."

"It's just, I get a lot of people wanting to write about me. Well, not me, but my plight."

"Well, not me. Not guilty. I'm a doctor."

Her stance softens, as so often happens when I play the medical card to strangers. It's the most trusted profession and comes with many presumptions, including that I am kind.

"Trust me, I'm a doctor, right?" she jokes and we both laugh. But then, just as quickly, she shakes her head.

"No, sorry."

I am crushed and about to plead.

"Not Selfridges, anyway," she continues.

"Oh?"

"They're not keen on people like me."

I grimace at this. "They are, if you're with me. They have a salt beef-"

"I am not going into Selfridges," she states firmly.

"No, okay then, fine."

"And I'm a vegetarian anyway."

I congratulate myself on my earlier judgement.

"Right then, somewhere else? Somewhere less stuffy?"

Again, she shakes her head.

"We could just walk?" she suggests.

"Err…" I am relieved. And I get it, too. Walking, she can remain in her environment: on the streets.

"Sure. Walking is great. Why not?"

"And we could find a place to sit, if you like?" she adds.

"Right."

I hope she doesn't mean a doorway or the pavement. I might not ever get up again.

"Portman Square? Do you know it?"

I don't particularly, even though it is close to my practice and where I live. I almost certainly will have clients who live on or around the famous quadrangle.

"It's not very far. There's a bench there that I use. I use it to think."

A square. A bench. A place to think. It all sounds so naff, like a romantic comedy.

"But only if you have time?" she asks. "You have a plane to catch, right?"

Panicking a little, I check my phone and read Deborah's text. Thank goodness for the flight change.

"No, it's fine. I have time. And I would like to sit with you, thank you very much."

"Okay then. But only on one condition…"

I chuckle at her manner and sense of poise; stating her terms and negotiating with one of the world's best paid physicians.

"And what is this condition?" I ask in a fatherly tone.

"That we share."

"What, the bench?"

"No, my bun."

"Oh?"

"Non-negotiable."

"Okay then, sure."

She smiles.

"I'm Gabriel, by the way."

She looks at me curiously. "That's a nice name."

"Yes, I suppose it is. Thank you."

"Hello Gabriel, I'm Catherine." We shake hands and immediately I feel a well of panic. I am grateful to see that she is wearing gloves but, with the fingers cut off at the knuckles, her filthy nails are exposed and completely at odds with my hygiene neurosis. I like to avoid all unnecessary contact like handshakes, preferring a general wave and hello. Door handles are a problem too. I use my sleeve when possible and always in a lavatory, plus I carry my disinfectant gel with me everywhere. Having shaken hands, I am desperate to use my gel now but I resist. The bun eating will be a challenge too but I hope that she will forget her terms once she sees it. I am still hungry but presumably not as hungry as her.

Our conversation is rather stilted but the walk to the square is mercifully short. We make an unusual couple and I notice a few bemused looks from passers-by. Finally, we reach the square and I look for a bench. There is only one that I can see and it is presently occupied by an elderly Chinese couple, tourists most likely. The bench has room for four people but this will feel uncomfortable and goes against bench etiquette. Benches are not like train seats; they can be fully claimed and, in some instances, even by a singleton. This unspoken rule is clearly not one acknowledged by Catherine, who walks towards the bench purposefully and as though it were free. My instincts are more polite and so I hang back.

"We can always go elsewhere?" I suggest lamely, but she ignores me and continues on. Just as we arrive, the tourists get up to leave. They smile broadly at the odd couple before them. I realise I must look like her father and nod awkwardly. She sits down and I do too.

"Well, that was lucky." I begin, happy to give my feet a rest.

She takes another sip of coffee then pulls out her bun and laughs.

"Blimey, I haven't had one of these for ages."

"No, old school me. That's why I got it."

She grabs the heavy pastry in both hands and tears it in two. Oh dear.

"No, no…" I insist.

She fixes me with an intent look which says quite plainly: we had a deal. She hands me my half and I notice some debris from her gloves is stark against the icing. My only option is to use my left hand to eat it since I have shaken her hand with my right. Not a great solution but something at least. She stares at me intently, almost like a challenge. Boxed in, I take a bite and instantly swallow, dog-like, keen to avoid any of the taste of London street life.

"Can I ask you a question?" she asks, politely.

"Yes, of course."

"Why did you buy this for me?"

"Err…"

"Do you even know?" she prods.

Her supplementary question surprises me.

"No, I don't, not really. Like I said earlier. Something just came over me."

"Because it felt like the right thing to do?" she probes.

I shrug.

"Yes, perhaps. Or because it's a nice thing to do?"

She doesn't answer but nods a little and continues looking at me.

"Wouldn't you agree?" I ask.

"Yes, but it depends on your motivation."

"Oh yes, I see that, but I can assure you that I do not have a motive," I reply quickly. She nods again.

"No offence intended, but what might I want from you?"

She seems satisfied enough at this and gently shrugs.

"Believe me, after the day I've had this is the last thing that I expected to be doing."

She is making light work of her bun and is almost finished.

"Like I said, I normally ignore the homeless. You know, no eye contact."

"Oh yes, I remember. On a moral principal or are you just mean?"

"Er…"

"You know, 'don't give money because they spend it on drugs and it just legitimises their way of life'. Or are you just mean?"

I chuckle at her directness. "I think that maybe I am both."

She mulls on this for a moment. "Well at least you're honest."

"Yes, I suppose there is that. But better if I was more charitable, though?"

"Everyone could be more charitable."

Catherine eyes my bun, noticing that I have ground to make up. I wish she would finish mine off also.

"And in return, can I ask you a question?"

She smiles knowingly. "How did I end up here?"

I nod and look a little bashful.

"You remember I asked if you were a journalist?"

"Ah, I see."

"It's what everyone wants to know."

"Yes, I can see that. I'm sorry."

"No, no need. It's the obvious question."

"Yes, but for some people on the street it seems that their story is more obvious and apparent-"

"Than mine, you mean?" She interrupts.

"Well, yes, because you don't strike me-"

"Why?" She asks quickly. "Because I'm called Catherine? And I speak well?"

"Well…" I hesitate.

"Because I'm middle-class?"

I continue to dither, worried that I have offended her.

"Yes, there is that," I say quietly.

She nods again.

"Yes, well, believe me. There is not one type."

"No?"

"All sorts and everyone can end up like me. We all have similarities, but I grant you, I am not atypical."

"No, as demonstrated by your language. Atypical…"

She smiles, seeming to enjoy my compliment.

"Like I say, all sorts end up on the streets, including the educated.'

"And these circumstances then… the similarities you mentioned?"

She sighs and takes a moment, looking at a bird swooping down for any available crumbs.

"Not exclusive and in no particular order?"

I wait.

"Mental health, family breakdown, unemployment, poverty, substance abuse…" She pauses. "Loneliness, violence, anger, sexual abuse, alcohol..."

I gesture my surrender.

Catherine finishes her bun and proceeds to lick her fingers clean of the icing sugar, something which I will definitely not be doing.

"And you personally?" I ask tentatively. "What about you? All of the above?"

She considers this for a moment and blows her cheeks out.

"Some, but not all. I'm atypical, remember? No sexual abuse, or family breakdown… well, not in the classic sense anyway. Dysfunctional though, so I broke away. Mental health? Certainly. I suffer from acute anxiety. Depression."

"And yet you moved away from your family?" I ask, surprised.

She nods.

"I am afraid that I'm a great disappointment to my family. Or my dad."

"But they love you?" I ask.

"Yeah, I guess. But it's complicated. My mental health underpins my entire life, always has done. And my parents tried. Got me to see people but it didn't help. You're not a psychologist, are you?"

I shake my head, "no."

"Then what? A GP?"

"No. Actually I'm a surgeon." I don't elaborate and I am relieved that she doesn't ask. Most likely I would have lied if she had. I gesture for her to continue.

"Pretty normal upbringing. I'm bright, did well at school. Got my degree, got a job, got married. Big mistake."

"Any kids?"

"No, thank god. I lost the house."

I frown.

"Don't ask. Turns out not all lawyers are the same. And my parents' told you so's weren't much help either. They never approved."

"That's tough," I agree.

"So, I lost my credit, had a breakdown. Lost my job…"

"What did you do? Your profession?"

"I was a buyer. In retail, fashion."

"Glamorous?"

"Ehrrr…. and in a career these days, you can't be out for too long."

"Because of how it reads to others?" I suggest.

"Exactly. Time out creates holes and holes need to be explained. Holes ruin a CV."

"Right, so you become a risk?"

She nods. "Yep, that's one way of putting it."

"And why did your marriage fail? Sorry, if that's not too prying."

"It is actually."

"I apologise."

"No, it's fine. I'm joking. What time is your flight?"

I take this to be her way of saying that it's too long and complicated to explain, so I leave it.

"Afterwards I had a series of disastrous relationships with men. And then some women. Less complicated."

I shrug, careful not to judge.

"Still no job, no income. I couldn't make the rent and being as I am, you know, the sort of person who uses 'atypical', there's pride…"

I nod and continue to piece together a jigsaw in my mind.

"Too proud to ask for help?" I suggest.

She sighs, a little mournfully.

"But what about your family?"

"Yes, I have lots of family. Immediate and extended. But it's complicated. My siblings are all successful. You know, married, kids, working. In-line and onside, you know?"

I shake my head, confused.

"With my dad."

"Oh, I see."

"My mum didn't have much to say. My dad is very religious which was a strain and the starting point, probably."

"And you're not? Religious?"

"Yeah, ish. Or I was. But never enough. Not for dad, anyway. And my rejecting his ways was my rejecting him."

I ponder this and I feel a pique of anger on her behalf.

"But couldn't you just lie?' I ask. "You know, just pretend. It's what parents do to get a school place."

She looks tired now, her mind recounting the pain.

"Like I say, it's complicated."

"Okay."

"Basically, I broke his heart and so mum's too. My siblings were angry with me, so what do you do? And I never imagined that this…" She gestures to the skies. "No one comes on to the street thinking it will be permanent. It's always just a temporary thing."

"And what about getting back?"

"What to, home? Bit late for that now."

"To work then?"

She shakes her head.

"No way. Professionally, I'm done."

"Really?"

"Fraid so. Too many holes. No fixed address. My First from Durham has been well and truly expunged. There's another word for you."

I smile but ponder what she has said.

"What did you read?"

"English literature."

"Ah, should have known. And, what about your siblings?"

She eyes me carefully.

"I'm the youngest by some distance. I hardly know the older ones and they know as much about me as they can cope with."

"That's sad to hear."

"Yeah but you know, they have their own lives. And their own stuff to deal with. Plus, they have an eye on the cake…"

This strikes a heavy chord with me.

"Their inheritance?"

"Yeah. Funny thing, money and what it can do." She adds as a sort of sign off and with it, Maurice Cohen leaps back into my mind but I banish him quickly enough this time.

"But I don't blame them."

"No?"

"No. Not really. Self-preservation is a very powerful thing. And whilst this is awful…" once again she gestures to the skies and where she lives, "…and not what I ever imagined, but right now… it's the least complicated option."

I shake my head, unable to understand. There must be a better way than to be homeless? I shake my head.

"But have you never heard of the prodigal son?" I begin to reason. "These are gender fluid times, you know."

She shrieks at this and claps her hands. "Okay, that's good. My dad would love that."

"But surely this can't be it, being homeless?" I exclaim.

She sighs heavily.

"There are degrees of homelessness."

I shake my head.

"I don't actually live on the streets. Or very rarely, anyway."

"Oh?"

"It's mainly men who actually sleep out. Some women do, but much fewer.'

"Right, so where do you live then?"

"Where I can. I don't have a home in the conventional sense. So, hostels, refuges… the odd floor from time to time. I move around. We all do. And very occasionally I might endure a night in an unlocked car. But mostly there are places for women. Salvation Army. Charities. A lot of churches. Ironic, isn't it?"

I chuckle along with her.

"It's way harder for men. Much fewer options. Lots of ex-services and ex-cons with various mental health issues and dependencies so places refuse to take them."

"So, they have no place to go?"

"Yep. They literally sleep on the streets. I wouldn't last a week."

Finally, I finish my bun, not caring anymore about the hygiene.

"And it's not such a leap, you know."

"No?"

"You'd be surprised. It can happen just like that and to all sorts. One minute someone has a job, family, kids at school, dog, but then…

She snaps her finger, "…something gives or snaps. One bet too many. One of the cogs stops and everything gets thrown out."

A young man walks towards the bench but reconsiders and veers off. He might have waited because I sense our time is coming to an end. The buns have gone and so too has the coffee.

I am enjoying our encounter so much even though Catherine creates more questions than she answers. Although I am horrified by her circumstances, I am somehow envious of her as well. Her manner and simple life, her acceptance and apparent contentment. Unwittingly, she has prodded me, enlightened me even and in this moment, I have an overwhelming desire to help her. It was always my intention anyway, to give her my change from the café, but now I am resolved to giving her all the money that I am carrying and I am even excited at the prospect. And if she does spend it on drugs then who am I am to judge? Half my clients are using illegal drugs and the other half are dependent on the prescribed variety; all in complete denial of course, but undone by their blood tests (which my clinic insurance policy insists upon ahead of any surgery).

I stand up and look down at her in a kindly manner. The way that a dad might do when dropping his daughter off at university for the first time as he looks into a young face full of excitement, nerves and jeopardy all combined. But there is much more jeopardy than excitement in Catherine's case. I fumble into my pocket for my wallet and ignore my sanitising gel. Too late for that now. The advantage of having nothing else in my wallet apart from a single credit card and my driving licence is that I can extract the money easily without taking my hand out of my pocket. I press the clutch of brand-new notes into her palm and I close her hand into a fist. She says nothing. Her smile is enough.

"I'm glad that we had this time together," I say. "I've enjoyed it more than I can ever explain. Thank you."

No doubt she is keen that I get on my way now so that she can get counting. More money than she has ever received I imagine, and I feel a pang of guilt at my virtuous pride.

"Thank you, Gabriel. I've enjoyed it as well. It isn't often that I get to have lunch with a surgeon."

I smile fondly and then turn to leave, a little overwhelmed at what has just happened. I walk on a few steps and it requires all my energy to stop myself turning around to catch a glimpse of her face and, presumably, her delight. I desperately want to but I worry that I might humiliate her. She has already thanked me and it is enough to know that I have helped her. That I have been kind. And besides, what might be a fortune to her is genuinely nothing to me; a bill in the restaurant I will be dining in tomorrow evening (and on expenses, naturally).

But, determined as I am, I know that I will succumb and turn around. I have to. I stop walking and pause for a brief moment and then I turn. Ideally other people might obscure her view and she won't see me. Or maybe she has already disappeared again as she did before? But neither of these scenarios play out. Catherine is still on her bench and in full view. She is staring directly at me, her mouth agape. I start towards her automatically, unsure of why, or what I am going to do. Hug her? Shake her hand? Looking curious, she stands up as I approach and the answer falls into my head. I know what I am going to do. As I am upon her, I open my arms and we embrace. As we hug, I free my right hand and fish inside my jacket pocket for the velvet pouch. I press it into Catherine's jacket pocket.

"Catherine, I want you to have this. It might be the difference, I don't know. But don't open it here. Do it somewhere quiet, where you won't be seen."

She sobs and sniffs.

"Thank you, Gabriel. Thank you."

"And have it valued. You must have it valued."

She continues to hold me tightly as she sobs. I can smell her street odour now but I don't mind. I hold her for a moment longer and then we finally release.

"I have a plane to catch."

"I know. Thank you, Gabriel."

"No, thank you. Thank you, Catherine."

CHAPTER EIGHT

In the taxi on my way home I steady myself and try to take stock of my day. There have been so many dizzying extremes. I peer out the window at the ongoing shoppers, darting here and there and all with at least one eye on their phones. I am pleased to be in my taxi and not running with the shoppers after the latest must have garment or gadget. Lots of words to describe them: folly, desperate, delusional… but it is not lost on me that I profit so well from precisely this dream-chasing. And with this, my introspection begins over again. I think about how my day started, with Bella, then Maurice and then Catherine, and I wonder what else does my day have in store for me?

With so many firsts it is not surprising that I feel so peculiar and unsettled. I have just had lunch with a homeless woman, not to mention given her something that is central to my existence; something so valuable that I wouldn't even have given it to my wife. Without question Catherine has been the highlight of the day so far, albeit an expensive encounter. I think of the watch and I shudder. Perhaps it is a good thing now that Maurice didn't cast his eye over it and provide me with a figure. But then I panic a little for a very different reason; worried that Catherine might be lying in a gutter somewhere with her eyes rolled back as some miscreant makes off with my watch. I reassure myself that she didn't mention her own drug use and that she didn't seem the type.

In the taxi and without cash, I am relieved to see the card payment facilities, and contactless too, which makes it easier to avoid tipping. I have already been generous enough today, thank you very much.

I fear that my extraordinary generosity is going to have repercussions; that it is going to come back to haunt me. I think of Maurice and I even manage a faint smile as I replay the moment when I handed Catherine my watch. Not such a squirrel now, eh? My stomach cramps sharply. It was certainly an extraordinary thing to do; a remarkable gesture, and not something I ever imagined doing. It was a reflex and beyond my control. It just happened. It is highly unlikely that Catherine will realise it's true value or spend its proceeds wisely. It might even harm her to own such a thing, since it makes her vulnerable. And now I am angry with Maurice Cohen all over again because this is all his fault. Had he just given me a valuation then none of this would have happened. I try to reassure myself: I am fortunate not to have a value because what could that have possibly achieved?

I decide it is much more productive that I concentrate on my kindness and the joy that I have created. I imagine Catherine's smile again and hold onto these thoughts as I stare out of my window. The taxi has stopped at a pedestrian crossing for a wealthy looking couple as they amble across Marylebone High Street. Better to give than to receive, as the cliché goes… but how much I would have enjoyed adding Bella's watch to my personal stash? My first AP. Was it worth more than seeing her smile? I feel a little hot now and I try to eschew any such negative thoughts.

They are not helpful and cause only pain as my stomach twinges again. With this, I resolve not to ever establish a valuation of Bella's watch. It would not be useful and it could possibly even kill me. Right on cue, my stomach twists again and this time, I let out a little yelp.

As a doctor, I muse on the physiology of this and a possible connection to my financial loss. The human body is a remarkably complex machine and for all our arrogance, physicians know next to nothing of its workings. I take my hand from my stomach and wipe my brow. It feels a little hot which is no surprise. I am highly stressed and I crack the window a little.

As usual, when I return home Judy is out and I quickly pack for my trip. I do so with some urgency because I have a financial loss to recoup and where better to go than Qatar? Travelling as often as I do, my packing is a routine that I have down. Our maid, Estella, makes things easy for me by having my clothes beautifully laundered and ordered in my large walk-in closet. I throw into my suitcase four pairs of socks and pants. Three tops, two pairs of trousers, pyjamas and a lightweight casual jacket. I have a dedicated and permanently stocked travel washbag containing everything I need and it fits perfectly into my leather multi-purpose case. It was ridiculously expensive and a rare luxury that I allow myself to use. Seeing my fellow first-class travellers with their elegant and practical luggage is what did it for me; observing these refined people retrieving their belongings with such ease whilst I fumble with my hopeless utilitarian bag where nothing is to hand and things get too easily damaged. I first saw what I wanted, unsurprisingly, in Selfridges, but eventually I purchased it online for a small but worthwhile saving.

I close my bag and consider myself in my hallway mirror. Today has been remarkable. A genuine watershed. I might even have saved a young woman's life. With this thought I enjoy the elation my medical colleagues must enjoy on a regular basis. I don't feel hot anymore and my stomach has settled also. Life is good. There are breasts that need altering and it's time to go.

My car is already outside for me but I still have plenty of time and my driver can wait. Despite my best efforts my mind wanders again and I know what this means. For all my self-assurances, I know the longing to find out how much the watch was worth will gnaw at me until it prevails. I take a deep breath and try to drag the memory of Catherine's happy face to the front of my mind, but it is no match for the forces against it. I try to reason with myself, because what good can it achieve? But it is no use. I set my bag down and pull out my laptop. Still standing, I flip it open and obediently it comes to life. My fingers flash across the keyboard and I suddenly I am waiting for the page to load. It will just be a benchmark valuation but I question what I am hoping to see... that the watch is cheaper than I had feared? This is the best outcome, although wouldn't this lessen my gesture of kindness? I decide that this is something I can live with. But what if my worst fear comes to pass and it is hideously valuable? The page finally appears. I do some cursory searching with my touchpad. A number appears on my screen and my eyes widen.

By the time I close the front door behind me my stomach is cramping wildly and my vision is blurring. My driver gets out of the car, rushes through my wrought iron gates and up my tiled pathway to grab my two bags.

"Afternoon, Mr. Webber. Are you okay there, sir?"

"Yes yes, I'm fine."

I get into the back seat of the enormous black Mercedes. I know the driver which is a good thing because he knows that I don't do small talk and nor do I tip. Nonetheless he smiles at me via his mirror as he hits the ignition button and eases the silent boat into the traffic. I take a series of big breaths and wipe my brow again, pleased to be finally on my way. To lose myself in work is the only thing to do in these circumstances. Like all my trips, I have already calculated what exactly this trip will net me, and from here, I like to work out my hourly rate and this is without factoring in any gifts. I am pleased too at the prospect of a long flight. I will watch a film, have a meal and then take a well-earned rest. If I can sleep that is, with this hideous number bashing about in my head.

At a traffic lights, I stare at a bunch of pigeons on the kerbside, some of which have no feet; burnt off by some acid deterrent. This makes me feel a little happier: I still have my feet and that puts my loss into perspective. Just then my stomach clenches hard and I let out a stifled yelp. The driver's eyes flash to me in his mirror again but he doesn't say a word. If anything, he might even be pleased. We pass a billboard featuring Roger Federer, the tennis God, looking pleased with his gleaming Rolex watch. Rolex, a worldwide brand for the nouveau rich. It is a billboard that would normally send my spirits soaring. But not today. My stomach tightens again and I begin to wonder if a pharmacy might be a good idea.

The value of Bella's watch continues to haunt me. The figure is burned onto my hard drive, an indelible number of hurt and pain. I should never have looked. So bloody predictable Gabriel. Weak. Even as I was stuffing the watch into her pocket, I knew I would find out its value. My brow is hot again and I open the window a little further.

"I can put the AC on if you like?" the driver suggests, but I ignore him. I gulp in the cool air and hope that the car might eventually pick up some speed. I remind myself that the watch had only just been given to me. It was hardly a loss. I mull on this for a moment but it is not very helpful. I already have many watches, most of which I never wear. Again, not helpful and my stomach twists once more.

By the time I arrive at the private reception area of London's City Airport, I feel awful and am dreading the flight. Bella's watch is forgotten now. All of my thoughts are on my stomach and my need for some antacids. With my two bags, I hurry into the airport. As usual, check-in is quiet: just one of the many advantages of not flying with the great unwashed. The lady at the desk is efficient and quick and I watch my hold bag disappear.

"Your flight is on time, boarding at your leisure from 6pm at gate 2. You have access to our lounge and a hotel suite across from the terminal."

I know this already but I nod anyway. She consults her screen for a moment longer. "Suite number seven. The key-code is on your boarding card."

"Thank you."

In Boots, I open the bottle of Gaviscon before the sales assistant can even hand me my receipt.

"Sorry about this."

I don't bother with the dispensing cup and glug my daily allowance straight from the bottle in one hit. I imagine the television advert with the graphic of the liquid overwhelming the fire in the oesophagus and stomach and I hope that it might do something similar in real life.

Outside the shop now, I realise that I need to quicken my step. I grip my carry bag and take the pace up a notch, alarm and panic setting in. Running at full tilt, I crash into the toilets and barely have time to open a stall and get my trousers down. I sit on the toilet as water cascades out of me. How stupid of me. Me, a doctor, linking my stomach cramps to my financial loss when I have clearly been poisoned by a blinking homeless person. How could I have been so bloody naïve?

Salmonella is a likely culprit, although I would not have expected a reaction so soon. This raises other more virulent and dangerous strains of poisoning like E coli, or even hepatitis. Although that too seems unlikely. I start to sob gently with both the physical and emotional pain of it all. A perfect storm. Why me? Not only have I given up my beautiful watch, but I have been poisoned for my efforts. Where is the justice? I hear another passenger enter the toilet but I don't have the energy nor the will to try and dampen any noises I make. It is out of my hands. My midriff is akin to a cement mixer as the pain bends me double and forces my head between my legs. For whatever fucked up reason I am being punished and I resolve to never be generous again. Catherine's image is replaced now by Maurice. Maurice Bloody Cohen and his grubby little face. God, how I hate him. I cannot describe my loathing for the little man and I imagine how I might exact my revenge. Fire-bombing his shop? One petrol rag through his letter box and I could watch his entire life go up in smoke. No doubt I will be caught and go to jail. It will mean the end of my career of course, but so what, because it will be worth it.

Sometime later, I don't know how long, I exit the stall. I am normally ruthlessly efficient in a toilet but today I have taken much longer; maybe even twenty acutely painful and awful minutes. I am dehydrated and feel as though I have passed a bottle of Domestos extra thick. This is a thing nowadays: men are bleaching their arses. Imagine! I practically crawl into a branch of WH Smiths. Only now I realise that I did not make it to the toilet in time as I had thought. My left trouser leg is wet and one of my shoes has taken a good splattering. I buy a bottle of water and drain it instantly.

With as much dignity as possible, I march through the terminal towards the exit and for the apartments across the street. I need some privacy and a place to have a shower.

CHAPTER NINE

Some hours later I wake with a start. I don't know how long exactly I have been asleep but immediately I panic because I can sense that all is not well. Something feels off. I am delirious, naked and lying on an unfamiliar bed. What time is it? I scramble for my watch or my phone but I can't find either. Why would I have taken my watch off? Have I been robbed? How long have I been asleep?

I get up heavily and stumble, my knees sore and creaking. My head pounds. Everything aches and I have a raging thirst. I have never been so thirsty before. My bottom remains sore and my throat rasps. Slowly, my mind clears and I begin to piece things together. Shit. My flight. Jesus Christ, my flight.

I find my watch on the dresser and as I stare at it, my panic and bewilderment grows. The small hand points to the seven, but which seventh hour? Morning or evening? Stumbling over to the window, I pull at my curtains and the room fills with bright sunshine. But this does little to enlighten me because it is May, meaning it could be morning or evening.

I grab the desk phone and call reception.

"Good morning, sir."

I scream and drop the phone. I have missed my flight. Fuck. I slump back on to my bed. How can this be? Can I really have slept for almost twelve hours straight? The implications are truly horrendous. My gilded clients failed.

My blasted mobile phone won't turn on and I am searching for my fucking charger when I am distracted by a knock at the door.

"Housekeeping."

My apartment is in an appalling state. I peer through my spy hole at the distorted face of a woman from the Philippines or someplace east.

"Sorry, I have not been well. Can you come back?"

"How long?"

I don't know. A week?

My mind is racing. I gulp from a bottle of water that I grab from the mini-bar. It is sparkling and painful but I don't care. By now my phone has come to life and is beeping furiously; no doubt messages from Deborah and Judy. I grab the remote control and flick on the television as I access my answerphone. There are six messages. The first is at 17.39: – Deborah calling to confirm that I was at the airport and everything was in order. The next is from Deborah again with the same message at 18.00, adding that she is having a spa treatment and that her phone would be off. The next is at 19.00: Deborah sounds frantic now but I am no longer listening, my attention drawn to the television and a news bulletin.

On the screen is an image of an ocean at night. It is dark, mean-looking and foreboding. Then the screen cuts to a graphic of the same ocean with a red dotted line; beginning from London, arcing into the air and ending with a red dot bleeping mid-ocean. I stare at the screen and in that moment, I have a dull sense of knowing and dread. I continue looking at the bleep on the screen until it blurs and I know now and I shake my head. My phone vibrates again but I ignore it. Instead, I grab the television remote control and raise the volume.

"...we cannot know for sure, but it has now been almost thirteen hours since the private jet left London City airport and has not been seen since..."

My body slumps. There are so many private jets taking off from City every day. Thirty or forty I would guess… but my sense of foreboding increases. I know it. My flight has gone down; swallowed by the Black Sea if the graphic is correct.

"…there has been no contact with the aircraft in London nor with its destination in Qatar and at this time, any number of scenarios are being considered…"

The screen cuts back to a news anchor in the studio, a black lady looking suitably sombre. She continues with her script, explaining that the plane is privately owned and has a capacity for twelve passengers and four crew members. It is believed that eight passengers were on board but no names are being released.

"Let's now cross to Qatar, where the plane was expected to have landed some four hours ago…"

I close my eyes and try to make some sense of what is happening. I don't know how to react. My aches and pains have vanished, replaced by total numbness. My fellow passengers have perished. I should have been with them and yet here I am. Should I be ecstatic, or devastated? I don't feel either. I feel desolate.

In the bathroom I splash my face with cold water. It stings and shocks. I stare at my reflection and begin to recalibrate again. I look old and tired and not very well. But I am alive. I sense a burden of guilt beginning to emerge. I need to make some calls. Hopefully people will be worried, and relieved now to hear from me.

Rather tellingly, the first call I place is to Deborah and not my wife. She answers immediately and bursts into tears the moment she hears my voice - a good sign.

"Gabe? Jesus Christ." She shrieks through her tears. "Oh my God, thank God. You're alive?"

It is more of a statement than a question and so I don't answer.

Deborah is delirious which is heartening and perhaps a little surprising.

"But what? How? I thought you were dead."

"I missed it. I missed the flight." I start to sob now, the realisation finally resonating and overwhelming me. Deborah too, as she continues to process and make sense of what she is hearing.

"Oh, thank God. But Jesus, Gabriel, how? What happened?"

But I don't have the energy to explain or to keep up with Deborah who understandably is flapping.

"Have you heard from Judy?" I ask and again I get that feeling' the feeling that something is awry.

"Yes, I spoke to her. She's worried sick. I'll call her now."

"No, no, don't do that. Please."

"Oh, okay."

I pause to think. "I'll call her."

"Okay, yes, of course. Make sure she's sitting down."

"Yes," I chuckle, grateful for the light release.

"I've called your clients but I haven't managed to speak to anyone as yet. They had someone on the flight too and it's rumoured to be a close family member, so you can imagine…"

I nod and mumble something empathetic, but in truth I cannot make sense of anything.

"How come you missed the flight?" she repeats.

I take a beat and breathe out heavily. I still need to figure this out for myself.

"I'll explain when I see you."

"Sure. Of course. Well, thank God you did."

"I'll see you on Tuesday. We'll speak over the weekend."

I play through the rest of my phone messages and I'm fretful that Judy is not amongst them. The news bulletin is back on the TV with the story of my missing plane.

Room service arrives with a plate of fruit I have ordered and a pot of tea. I take the tea without milk and I pick at the fruit gingerly. I begin with the bland melon and I leave out the acidic pineapple. I am famished which I think is a good sign. As I scroll down my phone, playing over yesterday's events, I come to Judy's number. I hit the green button but I get her answerphone. I don't leave a message. No need: the call itself is enough. What might I add? Hello darling, I'm alive.

The clothes boutique along from the hotel is over-priced but I don't care. I have soiled my clothes and I am supposed to be dead. I return to my suite, quickly shower and change into my new clothes, leaving my old attire in the bin. I did consider that my checked-in luggage might have been an option because presumably it will have been taken off the plane, but I don't know the procedure and I don't wish to draw attention to myself.

In a taxi on my way home, my muddled mind continues to struggle. I stare out at the world and life in general, carrying on regardless of whatever happens to me or anyone else. It is an odd feeling to feel so grateful to just be alive; something we all take for granted, until it is too late of course.

There is grief also for my fellow passengers whom I did not know but still, we have a connection. And guilt, too. Why have I been spared? I think of Judy again and I fret. Something is wrong. A lump forms in my throat to accompany a painful sense of sadness. It squeezes my larynx and physically hurts.

I feel a tear emerge from my right eye and eventually it bursts. Salty water runs freely down my face and curls across my mouth as I contemplate so many variables and outcomes, none of which I understand. I am sobbing freely now and I don't mind if my driver notices. Through my passenger window I stare at a vagrant in a doorway with just a cold dog for company and I think of Catherine. I would so like to see her again. I will need to now in order to understand my circumstances, to see if she is okay, and also to thank her. I think of Bella's watch and its value and how my initial loss is now been dwarfed by my gains. If there is any relief at being spared it is not apparent as yet. I feel chastened and shameful.

I get home. A house that I love. Another immaculate Georgian villa that I bought almost twenty years ago. It is one of London's most beautiful homes and I am immensely proud of it and yet suddenly, it holds no allure. Judy is not home which is odd since her car is parked in the drive. The nagging feeling starts again. With my cup of tea and all alone, I sit in my exquisite drawing room. The wallpaper alone cost over twenty thousand pounds - something I didn't baulk at because I view my home as an asset; a deposit account that I can cash in and recoup whenever I decide. My mind continues to flurry. A gamut of conflicting emotions: relief, anger, joy, guilt, shame and above all, sadness. I breathe out softly. Where is Judy? My life has been spared and yet I have no one to share my good fortune with.

I call Deborah to explain that I am home and safe. She has heard from the clients but I don't listen to what she has to say. I take a shower, slip into a pair of fresh pyjamas and collapse into my bed. For a man who has slept twelve hours already, I am surprisingly tired. Shock, I expect. My head feels heavy and bruised and welcomes the soft pillow. But my mind continues to race. I have been reprieved and I should be jubilant but I am not. I am desperately sad and all alone and, for the first time in my life, I cry myself to sleep.

CHAPTER TEN

I wake after a few hours and lie still, all my senses on alert. I make a quick assessment and re-confirm my circumstances, that this is real, and that I am not imagining things. I am not dreaming. There was a plane crash. I am alive. I stare at my ceiling, my ears straining for any sound. I don't hear anything but I feel that I am not alone: someone is in my house and yet my instincts prevent me from calling out. Through the window in our en-suite, I spy the natty little Maserati parked outside and everything immediately becomes clear. It explains my sense of dread. I sigh and I wonder what to do.

I stand at the top of the stairs and listen to the movements of Judy and a man named Stephen Green, who I now know to be her lover. He is an able lawyer and, rather appropriately, a divorce counsel who enjoys showing off and being attended to. Hence his car, and the range of expensive watches I have noticed that he owns too. He plays at our bridge club where he partners his plain and mousy-wife.

Everything makes sense now, and I wonder whether I should have realised already? Maybe I did but was in denial. Or perhaps I just don't care. Quickly, I scroll back over our encounters as a couple with Stephen and his wife; looking for any tell-tale signs and then opportunities that Judy and Stephen might have created for themselves. Her weekends away with the girls and odd weekday evenings out to dinner, that might have aroused my suspicions, only they did not?

It is not a liaison so difficult to understand and my reaction is sanguine, verging on self-pity. Certainly, I cannot blame Judy nor be angry with her. I am so often away and even when I am home I am distracted and inattentive; more concerned with the content of my safety deposit box. Judy has womanly needs: to be loved and cared for. She will have been low-hanging fruit for a predatory man like Stephen, who I suspect has a few Judies on the go at any one time.

They giggle loudly, the way that couples do when cuddling. They sound jubilant and I wonder whether they know about my plane… and how bad my appearance will play for them both. Is it a macabre celebration perhaps at Judy's new-found freedom? Not to mention her gargantuan wealth. Of course, it might all be completely innocent; that, Stephen has rushed over to console a woman who has just been bereaved. I shake my head. This is not the case and I am curious about what to do. Shall I do the theatrical thing? Burst in angrily and collapse to my knees? But if she thinks I am dead, my sudden appearance might actually kill her.

I gently push the kitchen door open. Judy sees me. Instantly her face falls in horror, not relief. And now I know for sure. Disbelieving, her face crumples and her mind visibly scrambles. My heart pangs for her and the hurt that she is feeling. Her mouth is agape but she has no words. The enormity of what is before her is too confusing and momentous to contemplate. Stephen has his back to me and swivels, his face aghast and a study in guilt.

"What? How?" he flounders, taking in the dead man before him. I don't know what to say either and I just shrug. Judy starts to splutter lots of random stuff but makes little sense and I am not listening anyway. It's all pretty sad and desperate. She doesn't know what to do; to embrace me, to be pleased or to protest her innocence. I am keen to reassure her that everything is going to be alright.

"Jesus, Gabriel. Oh my God. You're…"

Alive? Yes, sorry. She can't bring herself to say it because it compounds her guilt.

"Judy, please. Don't worry. I get it and it's fine."

"I should go," Stephen announces firmly and Judy fixes him with a look that I have never seen before.

Judy and I have much to discuss but now is not the time and I gesture that I am going to leave too. I close the door behind me and immediately I hear a sharp exchange between them.

In my bedroom I am packing again when I hear the front door slam and I gird myself. I hear Judy charging up the stairs and moments later my tearful wife enters.

"Gabriel, I don't know what to say…"

Still, I say nothing.

"I am so sorry…"

I smile at her warmly, grateful that she is not bothering with the denial which will only make things more protracted and hurtful.

I walk over to embrace her and she collapses into my arms. She is a considerable dead weight as she sobs uncontrollably with pain and, I hope, a degree of relief. Still I don't feel any anger, only sadness as I realise what a failure I have been as a husband.

We break off and I gesture to my case.

"But where are you going?" She asks, perfectly reasonably.

"I don't know. Judy, I am not cross with you."

Her face changes now. "Well, you should be."

"Well, I'm not."

"Oh, fuck off, Gabriel, please. Don't play the hero, it doesn't suit you," she snaps.

One thing I am not in all of this, is a hero.

"A lot has happened. I should have died last night and now this. I need to think."

"Right, yes, of course. And me too, so let me help you. Let's understand it together."

We make eye contact and I shake my head. Our marriage is

over and we both know it.

"Judy, please… I am not angry with you."

I kiss her on the forehead and she hugs me again.

"But where are you going?" she repeats, more frantic now.

"I don't know. Somewhere close. Somewhere I can think."

Slowly, she nods her head. She is both the grieving widow and the exposed adulteress; our lives are a mess and she continues to sob as I leave.

I check-in to the Midland hotel, a little down from Marble Arch. A non-descript and reasonably priced London hotel, it will be fine for now until I can re-establish a sense of normality again. I book for three nights and I sit alone in my bland room. A double bed, a dresser, a mini fridge and a TV that I will hardly use. All wrapped in magnolia walls with bad art. None of the fineries that I enjoy at home but I do not care. On the bed, I lay out my clothes for the stay. My laptop, my bank cards and card reader, my leather purse containing my keys and a strong envelope containing my stack of brand new fifty-pound notes. My life before me?

I call Deborah and explain things as best I can to her volley of questions. I am scant on real information and she is not very understanding. She insists that I honour my appointment on Tuesday morning and reluctantly agrees to cancel the procedure for the afternoon. There is no more information on the jet: still missing and no information on the passengers, who have presumably perished. I ask Deborah to retrieve my bag from City Airport, ready for me on Tuesday.

I sit on my 'easy' chair, which is not very easy, and I stare out the window at another fine London day. Still, my mind will not settle; throwing up far more questions than answers and none of them straightforward. And in particular the most prominent question of all which I cannot face and I try to banish. My stomach growls with hunger. It is a useful distraction. I have not eaten really since the ill-fated flight, only a small bowl of porridge and with no recurring ill-effects from my poisoning. Even this presents me with questions. How to explain such a short lived and violent bout of food-poisoning?

I add it to my ever-growing 'to do' list.

For now, I concentrate more on tangibles and absolutes and chiefly, my missed flight and crashed plane. Scouring online, I am obsessed with information and my spirits lift when I read news that a wreckage might have been spotted somewhere in the Black Sea. But my doom descends again as explanations are called for and the same question that nags at me. I think of the freezing water and the ghastly fate of my fellow passengers; a fate from which I was somehow spared. One moment, settling into a long flight in complete luxury, browsing film libraries and deciding on fish or meat, and then in an instant, hurtling towards a watery grave. I hope that it was quick. And then the questions again. Questions I cannot answer. People will say, 'thank God', but this is not helpful. Just another reminder of the fateful circumstances I must try to understand.

Catastrophic mechanical failure is the likely cause but an act of terror has still not been ruled out. Still no word on the occupants and this will be key. The ultra-rich do not die quietly and no doubt grief-stricken families will be assembling their teams. The lawyers will be the only winners because no one is being brought back to life. Insurance companies and their executives will be meeting now, manoeuvring and preparing. And whatever is decided and agreed upon, it will be of no consequence to the poor souls on the seabed.

My first day of my new life then. I eat at Selfridges, (where else?) and retire to bed early. I sleep fitfully which is no surprise. In the morning, Judy telephones me and we have a strained conversation where she accuses me of being in denial. Maybe so. I tell her where I am and I request that she does not visit me or call again, for the time being at least. It is yet another warm day and I feel delicate as I set out for a walk, carrying a cashmere jumper just in case. I buy a sandwich from Pret-A-Manger; the plainest one they have, and take a black coffee into Hyde Park to find a bench. This is highly appropriate since this all began on a bench, but I am not hopeful that any revelations are likely to occur.

I think of Catherine almost constantly. A chance encounter that saved my life. Literally saved my life. Was this pure good fortune or have I been spared? There it is, that bloody question again. Spared by whom? And why? I wonder about her outcome also; not as fortunate as mine, surely?

A large white gull hovers in the air above me and catches my eye. To be as free as a bird, isn't this what we all aspire to? Freedom. It checks its flight as it spots my sandwich. Again, I am reminded of Catherine and the last time I gave up some food. Everything reminds me of Catherine and my plight. Beyond the persistent bird and way off in the distance, an airliner banks; off somewhere far flung with people on board, excited to be on their holidays, and others I expect just going to work. To the Middle East perhaps and on-board a plastic surgeon on his way to fill his boots. A vapour trail behind the plane is rather beautiful and I think again of my plane and its terrible fate. I think of the word, 'fate', which I do not believe in. I have no truck with fate and I discard it. Stuff and bloody nonsense.

It is a lovely spring day; the sort that can soften even the hardest pessimist. I observe passers-by and I imagine their lives and back stories. Tourists mostly. London is genuinely the world city: the sheer array of languages, cultures and appearances is remarkable. I see a Chinese family. A young, cool couple from Spain or Portugal or Greece or Italy... An American man on his phone, busy and self-important. A tall black man in a shiny suit with a diminutive but heavily fat wife walking behind him and staring at her phone. An attractive Asian lady, Phillipino or Malaysian pushing a double pram with presumably twin babies on board. The maid or nanny I would guess and not the mother. And I think of the twins in the pushchair and the likely good fortune that they have been born in to; the life chances they enjoy but won't necessarily take. As a plastic surgeon, I am well accustomed to patients who seemingly have everything and yet suffer terribly.

The nanny bends forward to fuss over one of the babies and I speculate about their parents and her employer. Most likely an older couple, I decide. A house in Mayfair. Recently married and first-time parents, they have hastily and expensively conceived twins with the help of my colleagues in Harley Street. Assisted conception and assisted delivery too, I shouldn't imagine. Too posh to push and the pretty mother is back in the gym post-haste with other colleagues of mine on hand to offer more immediate solutions like a quick nip and tuck. And yet they still have worries of their own; worries every bit as real as anyone else's. I might be flat wrong of course, but I congratulate myself on my conjecture anyway; a welcome distraction from my own hapless plight.

I retrace my steps along Oxford Street to Portman Square again and I am pleased to see that the bench is unoccupied, as though it is waiting for me. I approach gingerly because I have high and unrealistic hopes about what it might provide.

But sitting down, I feel nothing. No connection and no inspiration. A disheveled tramp wanders toward me, capitalising on his crucial advantage of having made eye contact with me. Will I ever learn? Close now, he adds an outstretched hand to his pleading face but I shake my head and avert my gaze. He alters his path and shuffles on. I watch after him. He is bedraggled, much worse than Catherine's street appearance, and one of the homeless who really does live on the streets. This man has his worldly possessions with him and he sleeps where he can. His shoes are odd and one is without a heel. His hair is matted and a pungent odour trails after him. He is completely lost. Try explaining to him that all problems are relative and I feel chastened. And yet, I don't have the same compunction to act; to chase after him, to help and engage, which I suppose is an answer to a question that has been nagging me since my reprieve. Why then did I feel such a need to help Catherine? As a scientist I have spent my life dealing with absolutes and certainties. Binary issues with specific solutions. Yet I am now faced with a set of questions that no one can answer.

I watch after the poor wretch and I consider my rejection of him. The old Gabriel Webber remains alive and well it seems. Or more accurately, alive but not so well. The man shuffles more than he walks - and not just because he is missing a heel - with his furtive hand out-stretched like an opportune fish hook. But there are no bites and everyone avoids him. I wonder where he is heading. To see friends? To be with other homeless people because it is safer in numbers? Or, more likely, he is just walking aimlessly until he settles someplace, too exhausted to continue. What a pitiful existence. Once a babe in arms and presumably loved, but now all alone, reduced to nothing. Suddenly, I feel a connection with him.

I follow him with my gaze until he is completely obscured by oncoming pedestrians. In a city of millions, it is the last I will ever see of him. I think of Catherine again and my unlikely hope to see her again, if only to thank her for saving my life. Bella's watch has lost all meaning to me now. I am in her debt again and I must try to find her.

CHAPTER ELEVEN

On Tuesday morning, I leave my hotel after breakfast and walk the short distance to my office on Langley Street. Deborah observes me warily as I enter. She is right to look concerned because her boss is now in full-blown crisis and seems unable to resume his life as it was.

"Gabe, hi. So good to see you. How are you feeling?"

She rarely calls me Gabe and we embrace affectionately as I mutter something and I end jovially that it feels good to be alive, hoping that this might end her line of enquiry. It does not.

"So, awful?" It is a statement but delivered as a question, which I decide to ignore.

"Yes, it is."

"So, what happened then?" she asks bluntly. I blow my cheeks full. Where to start? "How come you missed your flight?"

It is a reasonable question but the truth is… what? That I felt compelled to have lunch with a homeless woman who poisoned me and in doing so, kept me off an ill-fated private jet? Easier to say nothing. I just shrug.

My silence is unsatisfactory and Deborah is happy to wait. And she might have a point - it might be a good thing to offload with whatever I have. I am conscious that I have hardly spoken with anyone since meeting Catherine, or at least, nothing beyond cursory conversations, including with Judy and the people I met at the women's hostels I visited yesterday; none of whom provided much hope of me finding Catherine.

Staffed by women and for women, the refuges I have visited so far have all drawn blanks. Their immediate tone is one of suspicion and even hostility, which is understandable; the assumption being that I have either malevolent intentions or guilt to assuage. Why should they help me? And then there is the data protection hurdle which no one can straddle.

"Do you want to talk about it?" Deborah asks, softening her enquiry to a plea. I smile and shake my head. Deborah will be a difficult person to explain my circumstances to, especially the section where I part with a valuable gift to a complete stranger. As well as the obvious hurt, it might arouse her suspicions also. And this homeless woman was attractive woman, you say?

"Perhaps later." I suggest as I point to my office door. "What time is she due?"

"Ten thirty. Mrs. Jane Asher."

My eyes narrow at the famous name but Deborah heads me off.

"Not that one. Her notes are on your desk."

"Great, thanks Deborah. Thank you."

She shrugs, no problem.

"Gabriel?" she calls after me.

"Yes."

"Is everything okay?"

I take a moment.

"No, not really. Things are different now… I think." It is the first time that I have said this to anyone or even to myself. But it is the truth, even if I cannot explain it. Not yet anyway.

"Right, well. It must have been a real shock."

"Yes. It still is."

She softens a little at this. Her old boss will return - just give it time.

"And is there anything I can do to help?"

"No. I don't think there is."

She sighs heavily.

"Judy called."

I nod, realising that she already knows what has happened in my marriage. As my PA she has liaised with Judy frequently over the years and they have developed a relationship of sorts.

"Yes… and there's that. Awkward."

Deborah looks mournful.

"Gabriel, I'm so sorry."

"No, no, don't be. Judy will be fine. I'm going to make sure of it."

Deborah goes to reply but I wave away her sympathies. And then something occurs to me.

"Actually, there is something you might do for me…"

Her face brightens. "Sure. Anything."

"Could you get a list of all the women's refuges in and around London? Centrally, to begin with I think."

At this her shoulders slump.

"Women's refuges?"

"Yes. Something has happened. But it's difficult to explain."

"Right…" Her compliance now seems to be contingent on further information.

"I'm looking for a young woman."

Deborah fails to hide her surprise.

"In a refuge?" she asks.

"Yes."

"You want to find a woman in a refuge?"

"Yes, that's right. I've been to a few already. Data protection is a problem."

Deborah fidgets now, hoping that this is not related to my marriage breakdown.

"Any woman or a specific woman because there are-"

"Yes, yes, I've met her already."

"Right. And does she have a name?"

"Oh, yes, of course. Catherine."

"Catherine?"

"Yes."

"Just, Catherine. And does she have a surname?"

I sigh and realise how ridiculous this sounds and why Deborah is staring at me, agog.

"With a C?" she asks pointedly.

This would be my guess. More modern. But of course, this too I can't say for sure.

"I don't know. Might be a K..."

There is another awkward moment but thankfully I am saved by the bell. Ms. Asher has arrived. I gesture to my office with a glance.

"I'll give you five minutes to look over her notes."

"Yes, good, best have a read."

I glance at my prospective patient's notes. My spirits plummet. Jane Asher is in fact Jaynne Asher, an American living in London. I am tense. The ridiculous spelling of her name grates on me more than it should. I already know Jaynne well enough, having met so many women just like her. She is thirty-four. She is not married but wants to be. I continue reading the notes and nod to myself, 'engagement, recently called off.' Her fiancé was possibly scared off by her rail thin mother. Her parents will be expensively divorced and the dad, a businessman, a lawyer or a Wall Street guy, will have a new wife only a few years older than his daughter. Thinner, and more attractive. Jaynne is an only child. She has had an expensive education but now has bleak career prospects. I look at the polaroid of Jaynne. Her Christian name is unfortunate because she is as plain as a bus. Currently working a non-job in PR, she is miserable and probably depressed. And she thinks that a new pair of boobs is the solution. I sigh heavily.

I welcome Jaynne into my large corner office, which has lovely views on two aspects. We shake hands and I point her towards an elegant chair. Jaynne is a simple read; as easy as the front page of any of our red tops. Pleasantries over, Jaynne is very soon naked from the waist up so that I can examine her. She has perfectly agreeable breasts already. Shapely enough, not too large or heavy, and well-proportioned for her rather agricultural frame.

"I'd like guys to notice them."

'I want guys to notice me' is what she means. I want to be married. I want to be happy. I nod but I don't say anything. She takes on an appealing expression and I know what is coming next.

"I was due to be married last fall."

Oh dear.

"I see."

"But my fiancé had other plans."

Empathy is not one of my talents. Even when I try, my wife tells me that my body language always betrays me.

"It runs in my family, it seems." Jaynne continues. "My family is not big on marriage."

I say nothing.

"My parents divorced…"

I allow myself a congratulatory moment for my prediction but it doesn't buoy me much because I cannot help her. Jaynne doesn't need surgery. She needs counselling. Better still; a new life and a new family. I suspect that she has few real friends, rather a new best friend every year. It is difficult to quantify but loneliness is the cruelest killer of them all and I should take note. A statistic I am aware of (but do not publicise) is the proportion of my patients who go on to develop suicidal tendencies; far higher than the national average - and Jaynne fits neatly in to this category. Suddenly I don't need to feign empathy anymore as my own circumstances present themselves. I recall my emptiness on seeing the tramp in Hyde Park and even envying him for his community. This is a heavy revelation to me and perhaps a breakthrough towards my own recovery; acknowledging that for all my obvious success, that I am isolated and desperately lonely.

"How big should I go?" Jaynne asks and snaps me back. Her question requires an objective answer. DD used to be the go-to size. Whilst you're on the slab… but things are not so simple anymore. The operation carries significant risks, not least from general anaesthetic. For Jaynne, it will be very painful, but nothing compared to the hurt she experiences when, after her excruciating convalescence, her white knight remains a no-show.

"And should I change their shape? You can do that, right?"

Her breasts are a fine shape already and so this is a significant moment for me. For the first time in my career, I decide that I am not going to operate. I cannot lie to this woman and take her money. I open my desk drawer and locate a series of business cards, quickly finding the one I need.

"I am going to recommend a colleague of mine who I think can help you better than me…"

"Oh, but I've been told that you're the best? You're the most expensive anyway, which is good because my dad is paying. He's a lawyer."

All I need now for a full house is his young, fit girlfriend, but I don't cheer and it only strengthens my resolve. I hand her the card and I wait for it to register.

"A shrink?" she shrieks.

"Doctor Andrews is a rather brilliant man," I lie.

"Fuck you. You think I need a shrink?"

"I just think that there are better options for you."

She is crying now and I consider calling in Deborah, who will be better at consoling her.

Jaynne stands up angrily. "Screw you, buddy. I came here to have my tits fixed."

"But they're not broken. Your breasts are fine."

"But guys like big tits- "

"No, only some men do. And they're idiots."

Her mouth is agape and so is mine.

Jaynne flees my office, her hopeless threats to sue me quickly replaced by the ire of my assistant. Deborah is aghast.

"For fuck sake, Gabriel. What's gotten in to you?"

"I can't help her."

"What?" Deborah glares at me. "Did you really just say that?"

"It's the truth."

"And? So, what? You're the boob guy, remember?"

I shrug but Deborah is through with my emollience.

"So finally, we have it then?" Deborah announces, being deliberately obtuse.

"Meaning what?" I ask obligingly.

"We've found something that the great Gabriel Webber cannot afford?"

I gesture for her to explain.

"A conscience, Gabriel. A bloody conscience."

This stings because I can see her point.

"Gabriel. We are a cosmetic breast surgery."

"Yes, I am aware of that, thank you."

"Right, and we do what people want us to do. We don't force anyone."

"Don't we?" I ask. I think of the adverts I place and the images in glossy magazines. But I admire her honesty and her sense of poise also.

"Right, so what happens now then?" she asks. Her self-interest is becoming evident.

"Deborah, I know that this is a shock. It's a shock to me."

"Yeah, I'll say…"

"But whatever I decide, I will ensure that anyone close to me is well accounted for." I am reminded of my similar conversation with Judy. Deborah, too, appears to be relieved. She might be surprised that I consider her as someone close to me. If only she knew.

"So, what about tomorrow then?"

A perfectly reasonable question and, in my flux, I had not even considered it. I look up at her fretfully, like the child holding cricket bat amongst the shards of glass.

"I am not able to be here tomorrow."

"What!" Deborah screams.

I wince. "I am unable to work."

"But what will I tell them?"

"I don't know, tell them I'm on holiday."

"Don't be ridiculous. You're booked months, sometimes a year in advance!"

"Yes. I am aware of that."

"A sabbatical then?" she suggests. "Just like that?"

"Yes, if you like?"

"Don't be so bloody ridiculous."

"Deborah, I just don't know. I don't know anything at the moment. I'm in shock."

"Well, that makes two of us."

"I need time," I offer. "Time to think." I cringe at how clichéd I sound. It's a wonder that I've managed to avoid talking about needing more space, or a 'safe space' even to use the modern parlance.

She breathes out heavily. It is a lot for her to take in. Her world, too, has been up-ended because there are other breast surgeons and her cushy job is being jeopardised.

"I'm sorry."

She takes another beat.

"Well, it was not an ordinary occurrence, I suppose. What happened to you…" she suggests.

"No, it wasn't. Who knows, maybe I'm grieving?"

She doesn't look convinced but she manages not to say so.

"And until I get back to work, whenever that is… Until then you will be paid in full. That is a promise."

Immediately, she softens. A faint smile even appears and quickly broadens.

"Well, thank you. That is good to hear. Thank you."

"Don't mention it. It's the least I can do for you."

She nods her head, thank you.

"And in the meantime, is there anything I can do?" she asks.

"Did you get a list of the hostels for me?"

CHAPTER TWELVE

My efforts online with the official website are completely fruitless and so I am reduced to the alumni association of Durham University. Like most entities these days it has a website with all sorts of facilities including 'search' and 'help'. But nowhere on the site is a bloody phone number so that I might speak to an actual person. And the online enquiry facility was never going to be easy to complete.

Christian name? It could be Catherine, Katherine or maybe even Cathryn. Or what of the American spelling, Katharynnh.

Surname? No.

Degree Course? English.

Date of graduation? Er… my best guess is somewhere between 1995 and 2010…

Unsurprisingly, my first submission is rejected altogether, due to 'insufficient data entry' and so I apply again, this time with the barest fictional information. The next day I receive a reply email and crucially with a phone number.

"So, you aren't looking for a John Bridge then?"

"Er, no."

"Then why did you say that you were?" the person from Durham Alumni asks, perfectly reasonably. "On the form that you submitted-"

"Yes, I know what I submitted. I've already explained this. But if I could just explain: I met a woman who attended Durham University who I am now trying to trace."

"And what's her name?"

I take a beat and breathe out slowly.

"I just have Catherine."

"No surname?"

"No. Which sounds ridiculous, I know. But-"

"Without a full name I can't help you,"

"She studied English. Could you do a search-"

"No. Not without a name."

The line cuts off and I stare at my computer screen. The hostels have produced nothing either. There must be a way… aren't there people who detect these sorts of things? In disbelief, I type 'private detectives' into my machine and instantly an array of search results appear. All first class with five-star reviews, entirely reliable detectives offering one hundred percent professionalism. I read briskly and quickly a theme of their service develops. Partner investigations. Relationships matters. Domestic trust issues. Confidential. Understanding. Discretion…

Utterly depressed, I close my laptop. I have a meeting to attend that I have been dreading and putting off for too long already.

Interacting with my lawyer is a considerable downside of getting divorced. His name is Russell Simons and he has been my lawyer for more than thirty years, ever since we set out in our respective professions. As my success grew I could have migrated over to a city firm - more in-keeping with my wealth - but instead I stuck with Russell because of his guile and his more realistic fees. He is as close to a friend that I have, although we rarely see each other socially and his apparent fondness for me is almost certainly motivated by self-interest.

Sitting in his drab and ordinary office just off Old Street, I explain my situation in as little detail as possible. Just that I am divorcing my wife and that he needs to make it happen. I leave out the personal crisis that has enveloped me although it will become apparent soon enough.

My old 'friend' feigns concern but, like mine, his body language fails him and his glee is quickly exposed. The news of Judy's infidelity is music to his ears. This is a payday he has long dreamt of; finally, his lottery win.

"Gabriel, what we have here, my friend, is all the aces." He might as well have rubbed his hands together. Suddenly I am dreading the prospect of sharing my intentions with him.

I have realised that my marriage was doomed long before my ill-fated flight and the revelation of the affair. I do not blame her for finding someone else, hence why I am gifting her such a generous settlement: because it is what she deserves.

Judy has had much to adjust to. She believed her husband to be dead, only for him to reappear and to lose him again, followed by the departure of her lover (who I believe quickly hot-footed it back to his wife and kids). Poor thing. Had I gone to my watery grave I wonder how things would have played out differently for her. She might have enjoyed the attention that comes with being the bereaved widow. And who knows, Steven might have even hung about to assess the extent of his lover's new wealth and how much more attractive this makes her. And given my generous intentions, I wonder if he might yet come sniffing back…

My bout of food poisoning has saved my life but ruined Judy's. How sad for us both. We met a few weeks ago at my hotel and it was pitiful. She had called and insisted that we met. She apologised and sobbed and suggested that we make another go of our marriage. She became angry when I refused and explained again that I was not angry at her. 'Why the hell not', she had demanded to know. It grated on her that I could forgive her so readily, but she softened quickly when I explained my intentions for our divorce.

Russell, however, could not be happier with the situation as it stands. Judy's adultery will cost her dearly, increasing my size of the cake and his slice also.

"Unless I decide not to cite her adultery," I throw in casually. For a moment I think Russell is so excited that he has not heard, but then his mood alters a little and he shifts.

"What did you say?"

I repeat myself and at first, he laughs but then quickly stops.

"Why would you do that?"

It's a good question and yet another one I cannot adequately answer.

My reasoning for not capitalising on Judy's adultery is complex. Her timing to see her lover on the day her husband supposedly died is appalling and yet any guilt she feels is more than matched by my own shortcomings as a husband. I suspect also that I might be trying to punish myself. Aren't we all prone to a little masochism?

Russell is still waiting for an answer but he will need to be patient. I am not the same client he has known for all these years. Something is afoot. I am turning away highly lucrative patients and I am about to relinquish a significant amount of my wealth. A watershed and a sea change combined.

I am now a different man, and if this sounds pretentious or clichéd then so be it. I am different. My life has been exposed as dysfunctional. It does not work. I explain this to Russell as best I can but I am scant on details. He says nothing at first, just stares at me.

"What are you, a lookalike? Where's Gabe? What have you done with him?"

I chuckle.

"Gabriel, look…" he begins kindly, choosing his words carefully. "You've been under a lot of strain-"

"Yes, I have. But it's not that."

"Yes, it is," he fires back quickly.

"No, this is something else."

"Is it?"

"Yes."

"What? That you've lost your mind?"

"No-"

"Well, what then?" he quips angrily. "Because everything that you've just said is complete and utter bollocks."

He might have a point and I don't know how to respond.

"So, what then? Come on, you need to explain it to me."

"I can't. It's complicated..."

"No, it's not. It's very straightforward actually. Think of it like a cake-"

"I'm giving Judy our house," I state flatly.

This hits Russell hard. He slumps back in his chair, his eyes fixed as he tries to understand.

I nod my head just to be clear and I can see his panic welling within.

"Gabriel..." He pauses for effect, possibly searching for the right words. "As your lawyer it is my job to protect you, correct?"

I guess so and so I nod.

"Right, and since you are having some sort of mental breakdown..."

"No, no, my mind is fine," I lie.

"Err, no. No, it fucking well is not."

"Russell, it is my wealth and my life, and there is nothing you can say that will make me change my mind."

"But she's the one having the affair! You've done nothing wrong."

I grin at this notion and think of my private bank accounts, my security box and how detached I am from her.

"Because as your lawyer, I cannot countenance-"

"You will do precisely as I instruct or else I will find myself another bloody lawyer."

"But-"

I rather enjoy the release that this provides me with. It is how I should have spoken to Maurice, instead of rolling over like a patsy and allowing him to assault me as he did.

"My house and half my liquid assets."

Russel's mouth falls open.

"But your beautiful house... it's got to be worth-"

"I know what it's worth."

I know this precisely because I keep updated on nearby house sales and enjoy updating my net present value on my various spread sheets.

"But where will you live?"

This I haven't thought about yet. The Midland Hotel will be suitable for the time being; I have even grown to rather like it. Interesting how we humans can nest.

"I'll buy another house."

"Yes, but not like the one you're leaving."

I shrug. So, what?

"Well, you must have a figure in mind? Jesus, Gabriel, knowing you, you'll have done some calculations. What, three million? Four, maybe?"

"I don't know," I snap, "I haven't given it much thought."

"No, clearly. But you should. Because, let me tell you, three million quid sounds a lot these days but do you know what it sounds like to me? A flat. Is that what you want? After all those boobs you've done, to end up living in a flat with too much glass, a gym and a Costa fucking Coffee?"

But I don't waver. I can't explain myself and nor do I need to.

"Russell, you needn't worry about me. I will be fine."

The reality finally hits him. No doubt he is now calculating the cost to himself because of my new-found benevolence, not to mention the damage to his reputation as a lawyer. But these are not my concerns and my mind drifts off to Catherine once again and where this all began.

Russell snaps his fingers loudly. He is smiling now, as though something has occurred to him.

"What is it?" I ask a little wearily.

"You wily old sod."

"What?"

"I know you. It's clever and I like it."

I have a good idea what he is implying but I don't say anything.

"Half of what she knows about, right?"

He claps his hands together for good measure.

"It's a distraction."

"What is?" I ask.

"Giving up your beautiful home. It's to throw her off."

Admittedly I am intrigued now.

"Throw her off what?"

"Your stash!"

My eyes narrow but I remain calm, careful not to give anything away.

"Whatever it is that you've got squirrelled away," he chirps conspiratorially. His use of 'squirrel' as a verb is highly unfortunate and it throws me.

Russell is delighted with himself and waiting for my face to crack, admitting my scurrilous plan. But there is no such plan and we stare at each other like two cowboys in a standoff.

His smile vanishes.

"Oh, fuck. You're serious?"

I nod my head.

"You haven't planned for this all along?" He asks.

I laugh at this, a welcome release. The idea that I might have planned anything in my last month is wildly flattering and equally implausible. His look of hurt quickly returns. The greed in his eyes is not a bad reflection of my own. It answers our friendship question at any rate. He doesn't care about me at all.

"My offer to Judy has nothing to do with any hidden wealth. It is simply the honourable thing to do. She has been my wife for over twenty-five years. And there is no hidden wealth," I add defiantly.

"Right, well, thanks a lot. Because you're sending me into a gun fight with a fucking spoon."

"There isn't going to be a fight, that's the whole point of my offer. I don't want to fight with my wife or with anyone else."

"No fight?"

"Yes, that's right."

"Are you serious? You're rich! Of course, there's going to be a fight. There has to be. It's a divorce."

"Well, not this time."

"But you're a multi-millionaire. Your property alone…"

"I will retain my practice and the building."

"Will you? Because they'll counter. Bound to. It's what I'd do. Wherever you start from, they'll want more. That's the law."

This arrests me. I bite the skin on the top of my thumb. I think for a moment but then I dismiss it. Judy loves our home and will be thrilled that she can stay. Having kept her looks, she will hit the gym and make herself quite the catch again.

"And she won't stop there. Your practice? Future earnings? The law is stacked against men. This might sound ugly or even ironic my friend, but she is going to fuck you."

He is not my friend but nonetheless, I cleave to the word and appreciate its use. I have never seen him so animated and his parlance so 'street'. Too many American box sets featuring badass lawyers is my assessment.

I instruct him to make my offer and I ignore his continuous protests. As I get up to leave, he stops me.

"Gabriel, what's happened? It's like I don't even know you."

He's right. I am not the man he knew. My life has changed and so have I.

CHAPTER THIRTEEN

Given that consistency is key for clear thinking and lucidity, I am critically hampered that my life is seemingly so full of contradictions. At times, I see glimpses of my old self and I wonder if this is something that I should cling on to, as a sign of my healing and the prospect of getting back to work and normality? Or should I eschew the old Gabriel to embrace the new?

Today is a good demonstration of this as I sit in my favourite place on earth: my viewing room, with my entire cache laid out before me. A genuine treasure trove which, just a short while ago, provided me with only gratification. Its value remains but its allure has faded, which I imagine is progress. It is certainly a departure from the man I once was and yet I still have with me my spreadsheet, updated with a current value, and no intentions to sell or part with any of its contents. A contradiction then? A partial healing?

It is my first visit since the plane crash and almost a week since Russell informed me about the counter offer from Judy's lawyers. Something he did warn me about and which he was at pains to remind me of in his best 'told you so' voice. He was right enough, that my generous offer would count for nothing. The wants of people are boundless. Greed is insatiable and I should know. It was a good decision then to hoard such wealth for a rainy day, just like this one.

I am pleased to report, however, that my masturbation days are over; a blessed relief and a welcome departure from the man I was. The tawdry man, pre-Catherine.

This is how I have come to think of myself; pre and post-Catherine, and in the third person too. It might seem self-aggrandising, but the detachment helps me to take a view and to try to understand my new circumstances. The two men are not the same and I am highly attuned to any signs to indicate one or the other. But their appearances and how they manifest is not a process that I can either steer or affect. I am impotent. These events visited me and the effects of my doomed flight and my reprieve are beyond my control. Or perhaps this is just a cop-out; something I just want to believe because I rather hope that the solutions might just emerge or occur to me. And I have decided to simply let fate continue its course as though I believe in such a thing. Since it all happened, my only pro-action has been trying to locate Catherine, which is both desperate and pathetic because what exactly might I ask her?

I consider my only Patek Phillipe watch and recall the upset it has caused between Maurice and myself. I have owned it for over five years and never worn it. It has never even left this hallowed room. I read somewhere the lunacy that we spend much energy searching and digging for gold and then we busy ourselves burying it again. Fool's gold, as they say.

From my carry case, I retrieve the letter from Judy's lawyers. Despite the warning, the counter offer is a surprise. The letter is unequivocal. 'Our client refutes the charge of adultery completely. Furthermore, and for the record…'

Russell could barely speak when he called me and then practically exploded when I explained that I did not have any evidence of the affair. No photographs, receipts, hotel bills, DNA, sperm samples or anything. I just have Judy's admission and apology, which are just hearsay since they are now being denied. The counter offer is equally bold, suggesting in addition to our primary residence and half all liquid assets that a claim is made on 50% of my future income as a medical practitioner, property income and 'any further capital gain on any assets and investments made during the marriage.' The letter goes on, requesting full disclosure of all net assets and specifically asks for and I quote,

'...all bank accounts held in joint names, Mr. and Mrs. G Webber and full disclosure of any further accounts in the name, Gabriel Webber, both on and off-shore and any further funds and assets secured in safety deposit boxes...'

I am confident that this is a bluff. I have been so careful. Nobody knows, I assure myself. It must be just a standard requisition by reptilian lawyers hoping to swell their slice of cake. I probably should have this confirmed by my own lawyer only I can't because I don't trust him. The only people who know about my box are the people at the facility. And Maurice Cohen... Panic grips me. Not only does Maurice know about my box but he also has a fair idea about its contents. Instantly my mouth dries and I begin to consider my options and other ramifications. Maurice doesn't know my wife but the Jewish community is small enough and thrives on schadenfreude. My eyes narrow. Perhaps I should move my haul. Bury my nuts elsewhere. But how, hire an armoured car? Transport it myself in small batches and be robbed en-route by a moped gang? I snarl as I snap shut my brief case. This is not happening. So much then for a new man emerging from the wreckage of a plane crash. Much of the old Gabriel Webber lives on.

Using my phone, I fire off a quick email to Russell. Ironic how little time it takes to dispense with so much wealth that took so long to acquire. My email is brief; explaining that I agree to their new demands completely but that I have already disclosed the full extent of my assets. I have no plans to sell my office building and it could be that I do not ever resume my career as a surgeon. And I refused to concede anything further.

I imagine the trauma the email will wreak in Russell's office and then again in Judy's law firm once they realise that they should have asked for more. Such generosity is not just the genesis of a new person, not entirely anyway. Partly, it is to assuage some guilt but it bears some malice also. Deborah has been quietly digging and informs me that Stephen has moved out from his marital home. He might have been kicked out, but I wonder instead whether it might have something to do with the new-found wealth of his former lover?

Another family is about to be broken then. I interpret the moral indignation I feel towards them positively. I rate their chances as a couple at zero, and I reason that the more money they have to play for and indulge themselves, the quicker it will destroy them.

The heavy door of the secure facility is held open for me by the kindly guard, a black man who never stops smiling.

"Thank you, Mr. Webber, nice to see you again. Thank you for coming."

I am embarrassed because I don't even know his name and my strained smile is no match for his natural beam. I envy him for his obvious contentment and realise that of the two of us, he is the wealthiest.

I bid him good day and feel a pang of sadness because this might be the last exchange I have with anyone for the rest of the day. Everything I encounter is a reminder of my loneliness and my failings. Every homeless person I see is a reminder of Catherine and that I cannot find her. Seeing couples together, kids going to school, lovers in the park, even seeing the staff in a café with their in-jokes and shared mission... They might be on a paltry income but at least they're in a team. Everyone is happier than me it seems and I don't know why or what I can do about it.

CHAPTER FOURTEEN

My London hotel is ever busy, bustling with tourists who are a welcome distraction. People come from the world over to visit London, presumably at great expense, and it makes me wonder what I might be missing? When I was working it was all consuming. I did little else because I had no time. But now I have time and nothing to do. I am waiting for the fates to decide and miserable for it, which is why I need to force the issue and become an agitator. I need to start to make things happen, I tell myself during one of my frequent walks and pep talks.

The concierge at my hotel assures me that Hamilton is the show that everyone wants to see, which it is why it is sold out. The concierge savours the moment, enjoying himself as he explains that there are always tickets available if one knows who to ask and is willing to pay the right price. No doubt it is a nice little earner for him. I make his job easier because I need only one ticket and I can go anytime. My diary is empty. Later in the day, I almost pass out when faced with a bill for £700. He makes it sound as though this is a great outcome and that he's done me a huge favour, so I don't baulk and instead hand over my credit card. The poster for the show claims it to be a life changing experience, and it had better not disappoint because that is precisely what I need.

The next day and on my way to the theatre, I check in on Bovis Enterprises, another desperate initiative of mine to make things happen, but one which feels doomed. Barry Bovis is a private detective and, unlike his website suggests, has little to offer and is as evasive as ever. For every person in need, there are an array of 'professionals' with their services to offer. One person's misery is another person's lunch. Lawyers who chase down whiplash victims, life coaches for the unfulfilled, loan sharks for the poor, and plastic surgeons for the unhappy.

Barry Bovis is a one-man band detective agency and is perhaps the greatest charlatan of all. An ex-copper, of course, Barry is thick as mince.

"I did warn you," he says from across his desk in his hired, generic office space - complete with remote PA/telephonist somewhere else. Cardiff, probably.

"No, you said that you'd be able to locate her."

"Unless she's dead, is what I said." He wrong foots me with this and if his comment is cruel then it doesn't seem to have occurred to him.

"And is she?" I ask, not unreasonably.

"Well…"

"Have there been any reported deaths on the streets recently?"

"There are always deaths on the streets."

"Yes, but of a young woman? A woman matching her description?" Barry's face falls and my spirits rise commensurately.

"So, she's not dead then, you just can't find her."

"With just a first name?"

"Which you knew when you took my money."

"Half your money. And as it says on my literature…" Barry scrambles for his pathetic flyer.

"I just need some feedback. At the very least where you have looked?"

I wait a moment.

"You have looked, I take it?"

"Yes, of course I've looked. I've even circulated the information with my north of England office where she studied. York, was it?"

"Durham."

"Yes, Durham. Sorry, yes. But that's north, so my northern office are looking at that angle…"

I sneer at the notion that Barry has a range of further offices. His fat, wine-soaked face is a source of deep annoyance to me.

"I'm constantly checking with the hostels, people on the ground and contacts I still have in the force."

The force, really? Do we still call our police service 'the force' as they busy themselves with people who hurt other people's feelings with nasty tweets?

"And still nothing?" I ask.

"'Fraid so. Nothing yet anyway."

"And the pawn shops? You said that they were our best chance."

Barry shakes his head which I do well not to punch. I gather my belongings. I have a matinee to catch. Barry Bovis. I should have known from his name alone.

The theatre is packed and even in my plumb seat, as I feared, the experience is underwhelming. I dwell only on the negatives. The play itself is jubilant but I fixate on the experience of being in a theatre where the sense of community and belonging is so apparent. The entire audience is a series of mini-communities with coaches parked up outside. It is full of families rewarding themselves with treats for special occasions and milestones. Everyone, it seems, is here with somebody else. Even the story and the acting company is one big community, rammed home by the encore where all the actors, so antagonistic to each other during the play, reappear as firm friends to the audience's cheers of delight. As I leave the theatre, my fellow audience members are feverishly discussing their favourite bits and my loneliness is further laid bar. But I cannot dwell on this if I am to make my appointment with

Antoine Tambor a few streets along in fashionable and expensive Belgravia.

Dr. Tambor is my psychotherapist, which are not words that I ever thought I would utter. He was Deborah's idea and I only agreed to it so that she would cease from asking me so many bloody questions. Now is the vanguard for mental health; basking in the spotlight as everyone self-diagnoses and demands instant empathy and attention. What starts in America eventually hops the pond and so it seems with legions of mental health professionals making hay on our epidemic.

Deborah selected Dr. Tambor from a long list, I suspect because he is reassuringly expensive and has some illustrious celebrities under his care. That these celebrities remain neurotic narcissists and deeply unhappy doesn't seem to count against the good doctor but there we are.

During our first session and almost immediately, I realise that Doctor Tambor is inordinately over-paid. He does little more than listen to his clients unload their unfortunate lives. Nice work if one can get it. But five weeks later and I am close to offering Deborah an apology and Dr. Tambor a thank you. Certainly, my cynicism of him and his branch of medicine has rescinded as I begin to understand the value of sharing. A problem shared is not quite a problem halved because Dr. Tambor does not offer any solutions, nor can he answer any of my questions. But no matter: I have come to enjoy our sessions and as my faith and trust in him grows, so has my candour.

I don't know whether this is his skill or my plight but by our sixth session, Dr. Tambor knows practically everything that there is to know about me, including my problem with my hoarded wealth and my fleeting encounter with a street person called Catherine. The only thing withheld is my masturbation fetish which is too embarrassing to share. Besides, I am cured of it now so why bother?

He looks at me intently as he mulls over what he has just heard. At the very least it is a fascinating story and I am hopeful that I have shared enough to perhaps take our sessions from monologue to dialogue.

"Well, that is very interesting," he begins.

"Yes, and confusing."

He nods at this and takes a further moment.

"So, you've cheated death then?"

"Well, I survived."

"Yes. And it must be a great relief."

It is my turn to dwell now which I suppose is a response in itself.

"Or not perhaps?" he asks. "You're having doubts?" he probes and I consider what a waste of time our previous sessions have been, all bogged down in my marriage and my professional life.

"Well there are doubts, certainly. Lots of questions and few answers."

"Some very big questions, I presume?"

"Yes, I think that's fair."

"Like your purpose? A reason why you might have been spared?"

"Yes, there is that."

"Which is not so uncommon."

"No?"

"No. What you're feeling is insecurity and bewilderment and perfectly normal I would say, given the circumstances."

It is the first time that he has assumed and offered anything.

"You are experiencing the feeling of being spared and you are wondering why," he concludes.

Yes, correct. But I know this already and I am more interested in an answer.

"And, perhaps more importantly," he adds. "What you should do with it. The opportunity, I mean."

"*Should* do?" I reply, putting his words back at him. But he shakes his head.

"Should? That implies that I need to change." I state.

"No, not necessarily. But you said so yourself, your life has already changed."

"Yes, it has. Most definitely."

"How so?" He asks and, for the first time, he seems genuinely interested and not just a guy doing his job. But where to start on the changes in my life. It's easier to just say nothing.

"It's the why that bothers me the most. You know, why me?" I suggest.

He nods sagely. "Well, that's a question that we all want answering. The meaning of life and our place in it."

"Right, and what's your take?" I force on him. "Why was I reprieved?"

Immediately his demeanour alters.

"Well, if I knew the answer to that..."

"Sure. But maybe just try. Humour me. What's your take? Off the record," I plea.

"Well, there needn't be a reason of course. It could just be good fortune."

"Really? And the virulent food poisoning then? What, just random..."

He shrugs. This is not the romantic explanation that I am wanting to hear.

"But the tests were negative for salmonella and anything else," I restate to try and force him further. Come on man, you're the expert. I think I know the answer but I'd like to hear someone else say it.

"That it might have been something pre-ordained?" I finally suggest, bored of waiting.

"Like fate, you mean?" he asks, shuffling uncomfortably.

"Call it what you like,' I breathe out heavily. "Something planned out for me. By a higher force maybe?"

He is squirming now and, I imagine, panicking.

"Well, I am not a believer myself..."

"No, nor me, but you see my point?"

"Well, yeah, I guess..."

"As though, I might have been chosen?"

His eyes flash to his wall clock, no doubt to see what time is left of our session.

"Well, certainly, this is how some people interpret such things. And how it might play out, were we in a movie."

"But we aren't. We're not in a movie or a novel. This is real. It is my life."

"Yes, quite," he agrees.

"Then how am I supposed to react? What should I do?"

These are the questions that keep me awake. Questions that I know he can't answer either. His eyes take in his clock again but time is not his friend.

"Well, it's just a suggestion…"

"Yes?"

"But from what you've been saying, your wealth is very important to you…"

I nod, noting his use of the present tense.

"…beholden to, I think is the phrase that you used."

He stops now and lets the words hang. His inference is perfectly clear but once more, I am keen to hear him say it.

"Yes, go on."

"Well, perhaps there is a moral message here."

Another nod from me. Still you pal. Ultimately, I am waiting for him to insult me.

"You know, this might be a sign of what is truly valuable in life: life itself."

"Just being alive you mean?"

"Yes, and being healthy. And living in the west, being educated… And that being beholden to more worldly goods is not so productive. That it can be something that overwhelms us, almost like an illness and is therefore something to avoid."

And finally, there we have it. I knew this already but it's a great relief to hear nonetheless. His awkwardness is palpable and made all the worse by the fact that he is wearing an expensive watch. A Breitling, I think.

"But if this is the case, if it is a sign, then-"

"That's just how some people might choose to…"

"Yes. Fine. But if it is?" I insist.

"Yes," he concedes reluctantly.

"Pretty drastic way to deliver it, don't you think?"

"What do you mean?" he asks.

"Well, to down a jet full of innocent people in order to teach me a lesson. What sort of God are we talking about here?"

This has already gone way too far off-piste and, desperate now, he needs to put an end to our fanciful conjecture.

"I'm not saying-"

"Yes, I know what you're not saying. And I agree with you. But you see my point?"

"I do."

"But if it is a lesson? Then what I am to do. Sell my worldly goods and start following him?"

Dr. Tambor breathes out heavily and shakes his head.

"I'm not being fair, I know. But I'm not asking you as a doctor."

"Just my personal opinion then…"

I nod.

"Well, yes, you might do something with your money."

"Something else you mean?"

He chooses not to answer.

"Other than hoarding it or buying myself expensive things like watches?" I suggest.

A low blow from me and I can see that it connects.

"Well, everything is relative of course."

"But what you mean, is doing something worthy with it?" And finally, I lay it out.

"Well yes. That would seem an obvious lesson and a way forward."

I don't say anything.

"And you said yourself, you enjoyed giving Catherine the watch. Or at least, you no longer regret it?"

"And I still hope to meet her again."

"Well, quite. Look, whether we have a faith or not, the Bible is a book of great wisdom…"

I gesture for him to continue.

"And isn't this one of its central tenets?"

We both sit in silence for a moment, reflecting. His answer

irritates me and not just because I knew it was coming. Just because. Because it is just so bloody unhelpful.

I sniff to clear my nose.

"Bit clichéd though, don't you think?"

"Err…"

"And cheesy?" I add.

"Well, I'm not sure…"

"Multi-Millionaire, cosmetic surgeon dodges death and sees the light."

I let this hang for a moment.

"Like the plot of an airport novel?"

"Well, that depends."

"On what?"

"Gabriel, I'm not sure if this is terribly helpful?"

But on this, he is wrong. It has been useful to share and to hear some of my thoughts and fears reflected back at me. And if it is hackneyed, then so what? This is my reality and what I must confront. Right on cue, his wall clock chimes.

CHAPTER FIFTEEN

'Everything for a reason' is my current mantra and so it is that my session with Dr. Tambor is a factor in why I decided to take the meeting. My highly developed ego also playing its part of course.

On Friday morning, we meet in a pub just off the Grey's Inn Road. It is early lunchtime and even though he is a journalist, I am still surprised that he orders a pint of beer which he finishes in a few gulps. I go with sparkling water. His name is Rory Banks. He knows an awful lot about me but I am not flattered. I remind myself that he is a man at work. He wants something from me for himself and I need to be on guard.

He recounts the last eight weeks of my life and doesn't do too badly.

He makes some mistakes and fills in a few blanks, but he hits the main beats and I am keen to know who might have enlightened him. Sadly, the list of possible informants is not long: Deborah, Russell, Judy, Dr. Tambor and perhaps a few others through hearsay.

I ask him flat out, but he is unperturbed and predictably spouts the usual defence about discretion and protecting his source. I reason that this is nonsense. A keen and enquiring mind could have pieced it all together, it is not such a leap. My flight did go down. My practice is closed. My marriage has ended. And no doubt he is aware that I have famous clients, which I suspect is what really interests him. Celebrity is the new currency these days. But then he says something that unnerves me.

"And now you are taking on charitable works, I see?"

My eyes narrow. This is not something that I have told anyone, nor that he could know himself, unless…

"Have you been following me?"

"No, of course not. I would never do that."

I glare at him, playing back certain instances over the last few weeks in my mind.

"Then how the hell do you know?"

He smiles, pleased with himself, and makes a note in his pad. Had he been bluffing?

"It's not so uncommon," he begins and I feel insulted.

"How dare you."

"And I saw you."

"What, when?" I almost shout.

"Today. Coming here today, to meet with you."

I quickly retrace my journey and what he might have seen.

"I was walking behind you."

"So, you were following me, then?" I state defensively.

"No, I was walking behind you," he replies confidently.

I recall my engagement with a homeless man.

He smiles broadly. "Nothing to be ashamed of."

"It's my business."

"Sure, but its more than most people do. More than me, anyway. You should be proud."

I sense a patronising air and I fix him with a withering look.

"Is that right?"

"Sure."

"You do know that pride is one of the deadly sins?'

He shrugs. "Yeah, well, I don't go in for religion myself."

"No, neither do I."

"There's no problem then?'

He writes something further in his pad and I scold myself.

"What you did was very kind. I'm sure he was pleased anyway. What did you give him?"

"None of your business."

He smirks and doesn't push.

"I am not a supporter of modern-day journalism. You may have read-"

"The FT piece. Awful. A set up to frame their narrative."

This is a neat way of putting it. Bang on, in fact.

"But that is not what we do, nor what this piece is about."

"Fine. But nevertheless, I don't appreciate people digging into my life."

He shrugs. "Why?"

His question is so blunt, it surprises me.

"Because your life is a remarkable one."

Another curve ball for me.

"And what have you to hide?"

Err, plenty. But I say nothing.

"Nothing! he exclaims, "you have nothing to hide. You've done nothing wrong. And more than that. This is a truly fantastic story."

He smiles again, his confidence growing as he senses a breakthrough. My blasted ego. I soften immediately. He is right, my life is remarkable and my story is too.

"Our readers will love it. They love this sort of stuff."

Do they? Will they love me?

"Saturday edition, two thousand words. Readers will love you."

This is the clincher for me.

"And we'll pay, of course."

The money is unimportant. I am only interested in being loved and understood. This is wildly exciting for me, which I do my best to mask. The golden rule in any transaction or negotiation: never appear keen. The words will need to be sympathetic and I will need to have an input and say on the tone. Even editorial approval. Is that a thing? Suddenly something occurs to me. A path clears… or a door opens, whichever metaphor best suits. A light? I am in a tunnel and suddenly, there it is…

"I'm interested."

"Great. That's great news."

"But I will need to think about it."

"Oh…"

"I just need a time to process it all and think through the implications."

"Of course."

"I'm a very private person, you see."

"Sure."

"Do you have a card?"

I leave the pub in a fevered state of excitement; the kind that only comes with pivotal moments. I congratulate myself on agreeing to meet with the toad. How right I was. Everything for a reason. I am going to write this story myself. It is my story. I am going to write a bloody book.

The idea is intoxicating and being in complete control will allow me to drive the narrative. People will indeed love me but more importantly, I am in the driving seat again. No longer impotent, I am on my way to making things happen. Most excitingly, as I write, the answers to the imponderable questions will surely emerge and it is my responsibility to share my lessons with the world. A book and my life story is the solution. What a privilege and how exciting.

Back in the square and sitting on our bench, I enjoy taking in the scene before me. I cannot recall when I last felt so exhilarated. I am grateful to Catherine and I give her a little nod to her impact. She will feature in my book of course and I still live in hope of meeting her again. I have given up expecting to happen upon her on this bench but still, I enjoy coming here and the connection that it provides me with. I breathe in loftily. I think of the doomed aircraft and my inordinate good fortune. I fill my lungs again and feel my body tingle. I am so blessed. And not just because I am alive, but because of the story I have to share. A story that will be translated into every language known to man. It will be a sensation. Literary festivals will clamber for me and I will collect prizes across the globe. A Nobel prize, perhaps? Sales will be enormous. Unparalleled. A must-read. Which actor will be charged with committing me to celluloid? Hanks, Nicholson, Hoffman?

I amuse myself with possible titles. *The World Doctor?* Good, but a little grand perhaps. Or maybe not? *The Enlightenment…* no, too oblique and likely to be confused with the historical event. *A Doctor Heals*. Yes, this is good. It refers neatly to my own personal healing but is less strong because as a breast surgeon, can I really claim to have healed my patients? But no matter because my book will brim with wisdom that will heal and salve anyone lucky enough to read it. A book for everyone. A Doctor Heals is, at present, in pole position.

A Doctor Heals by Gabriel Webber.

I imagine the front cover. A photograph of me, sitting in my beautiful office. In a suit or a white coat. Actually, perhaps I should include my name in the title. Or maybe just my Christian name, as Gabriel is suitably rare, dignified and even spiritual. Again, it all seems fated. That my life has been lived out for a purpose which neatly excuses any of my shortcomings. Heady stuff.

'A Doctor Heals.'

It's a fine title but perhaps not worthy enough. Such an important book needs a more powerful title. *The Angel Gabriel?* I write this down and I smile. Could I be so bold?

CHAPTER SIXTEEN

A project such as this requires special circumstances, which is why I am hurrying along to Regent Street. I don't like being beholden to the Californian behemoth, but I see no other option. This book, in explaining my life, will also complete me. Or maybe it will just be the first chapter of a new life because there is more greatness ahead? I hope so and I make a mental note of this. I really should get a notebook to jot things down as they occur. If ever a venture calls for a little indulgence, it is this. A line in the sand. To mark the occasion but also because it warrants a dedicated machine, untainted by anything else.

In the clinical and minimal Apple store, I take enormous pleasure in asking the sales assistant for a laptop that is best suited to writing a novel.

A silly question, since all computers are equally capable and presumably it is the writer and not the machine that is the deciding factor to produce a seminal book. But I am free-wheeling now, allowing myself to be led. Everything for a reason! My decision makes perfect sense.

If the need takes me, then I will explain to the young sales person that I am about to write the novel that will change the world. And on the very laptop that he sold! It is something he will be able to tell his grandkids about. Like me, he looks like he needs saving. In his late-thirties, he is too old for the tattoos that cover his arms and snake up from beneath his tee-shirt, covering half his neck. A middle class kid whose parents must be ashen? If he is impressed by my confidence then he hides it well. He asks me a few cursory questions about specs but I deliberately give the impression of nonchalance and being pressed for time. I have a book to write and money is not an issue. Just get me the very best laptop that you have. Now.

He taps away on his hand-held device and quickly the machine is delivered by a female colleague, who is also covered in ink and has metal studs and rings all over her once pretty face. I pay extra to have the necessary software loaded on to the machine. Another indulgence since I already own copies but I cannot risk there being an issue with the licensing. I need to start work immediately.

In Selfridges, I finished my salt beef sandwich and wipe my mouth. The place is busy with shoppers. Mums and daughters bonding mostly, and other random people with time on their hands. It is noisy and not ideal for writing such a literary phenomenon but I can contain myself no longer. The story is bursting out of me. I take my brand-new machine from its alluring box, aware of people's eyes on me; if only they knew what is in prospect. Hadn't JK Rowling started writing in a café somewhere? No doubt people dine out on the fact they witnessed the birth of the boy wizard.

I wait for the screen to fire up and quickly add the necessary registration details. I choose a password: Pulitzer. Why not? Aim high.

The software loads and finally a blank screen presents itself to me. The possibilities before me are remarkable. What a privilege, I feel humbled. From an alphabet of just twenty-six letters I can create a document of profound importance. The book of our time. Up there with the Bible? I have a purpose now. A calling. My loneliness is forgotten.

I stare at the gleaming screen and type, *The Angel Gabriel.* Immediately, I delete it. At this juncture, I just need a temporary title. Something just for the purpose of saving the document.

And so, I begin again, the blinking cursor waiting eagerly.

"What is that I am asking of my readers?" I ask myself quietly. My mind races and plays with various answers and options. I begin to type.

Take a chance on me.

I stare at the words. First, I underline them and then centre them on the screen to see if this helps. It doesn't. It is a horrible title. Too low brow; the title of the biography of a ghastly soap 'star'. But it will do for now. It is just temporary and I need to get writing.

An hour later, I have drunk a lot of coffee - more coffee than I have wanted or enjoyed - and I have written very little. I leave Selfridges a little ruffled and deflated. Yes, writing is difficult, but how hard can it be, really?

Bloody hard, I soon discover as the next three hours in my hotel room are also fruitless. I might need to reassess my dim view of the arts. I need a decent start, which is hampered by not having a clear vision. Is this fiction or non-fiction? A novel? And what tense do I write in? Present or past? I have no idea. First person or third. Am I the narrator or the protagonist? So much to consider and to inhibit me. I just need to make a start. Allow the words to flow and let the form that best suits my story to naturally emerge.

A further two hours on and I am playing around with different fonts. Calibri (Body) has a nice look but Google is adamant that Times New Roman is the standard default for books. There are just so many fonts to choose from. Who knew?

Four hours in, I have written nothing, but I have made some progress. I have decided that I must narrate the story myself. 'I, Gabriel Webber…' will tell the world my story. I like this and so I make a note on a loose scrap of the headed paper that my hotel provides. And I will write it in the present tense, not the past. This will make it more real and force me to be honest, without which the book will lack any resonance and depth. But if I am so candid, won't my readers give up on me and my story? Quite possibly, so I decide that an introduction (warning) is needed and this is the foundation from which I can launch. One thing is certain; I will keep my wanking fetish to myself.

It is a chastening realisation that writing is so bloody difficult. In to my sixth hour and I have barely a page and a half to show. Eight hundred and ninety-eight words to be precise. I wonder how many words a book needs to be? Already I am beholden to my word count, every bit as compelling as a taxi meter.

I read through my introduction slowly. It isn't awful, but it isn't very good either. I notice that my tense wavers and I assure myself that this project is bound to be difficult. It needs to be difficult. I have a lifetime to recount and a mountain to scale.

I retire to bed in a mild state of panic, hoping that inspiration might arrive as I sleep. I have heard of such things happening, but I sleep badly and the next morning I am exhausted and with no such inspiration. Today though, I do not panic. I am a surgeon. I am calm and collected. Highly skilled and highly capable. Adaptable and adroit.

After breakfast, I pop out to WH Smiths and buy a beautiful sketchpad and a packet of coloured pens. As a scientist, I have a structured and ordered mind, and the way to access my creative side is by using pictures and mind maps, I decide.

Back in my room, I stare at my multi-coloured drawing representing my life. Lots of arrows and badly drawn images including a park bench, an angel, lots of dollar and pound signs and an aeroplane approaching a blue ocean. And lots breasts of course, which could double as flying birds. As such, the story before me is child-like and incomplete and I try not to panic. I assure myself that as I write, the answers will reveal themselves and that my life will complete. I hope so anyway. My laptop stands ready but instead, I reach for a yellow felt tip because I want to draw the sun.

By the time I see Dr. Tambor again, my spirits are seriously dampened. Writing might even be a skill that is beyond me.

Dr. Tambor, though, is very encouraged to hear of my new initiative.

"Well, I think that it's a brilliant idea."

"You do?"

"Absolutely."

"Only I don't know how it ends." The truth is I can hardly write the beginning either, but he dismisses such doubts easily enough.

"If I build it, they will come." He announces fondly and rather loses me.

"What?" I ask.

"Field of Dreams!"

I shake my head. "You haven't seen Field of Dreams?"

"No, not that I recall anyway."

"Oh my God, you need to watch this movie. Your ending is out there, you just need to be patient."

"And what if the ending is not worthy of the beginning? What if nothing interesting happens?"

"It will."

"But what if it doesn't?"

"Erm…"

"What if I live out my days in lonely misery. Who will want to read that story? No one."

I hope that he will contest this. After all, he's a professional in the business of making people feel better about themselves.

"Yes, there is that I suppose."

Russell, my lawyer, is not remotely interested. 'What the fuck do you want to do that for', are his exact words. His focus remains on my marital status and ironically, me fucking my wife; his vulgar expression, not mine and which I don't want to do on any level. The process of our separation is certainly galloping along anyway. It appears that family law has changed since Judy and I married and that divorce is now much more routine.

"Marriage is not what it was, I'm afraid," Russell moans. "I blame the blinking homosexuals. As soon as they got in on the act, it was always…"

I zone out, tormented again now. My sense of impotence is back with a vengeance.

"You said that there is something I need to sign?" I ask.

"Yes, nothing too important, only your bloody life away. Unless of course you've finally woken up?"

I sigh as I take the sheet of paper and give it a cursory read.

Given my sense of isolation, it is odd that I should be pursuing a divorce. Another contradiction to wrestle with, and yet I have no doubts that it is the correct thing to pursue. I hope that Judy can be happy again and I need to dissociate myself from everything pre-Catherine. I continue to read the document whilst Russell witters on in the background.

"… in summary, you are giving up seven million quid more than you need to. Give or take a few million. And I use the verb take quite intentionally, because it is exactly what Judy and her lover boy are doing."

It's a neat use of language. I wonder if he rehearsed that line or if it just came to him. I don't have such a way with words. This is entirely apparent to me now. Two weeks since my literary calling and my introduction is the only thing I have completed - and it remains pretty thin and basically, piss poor. A writing course is a good idea, but I worry that I will be the oldest student and too old to learn a new skill. Plus, I don't have the time any longer. I need answers and people need this book.

I dial down my expectations. Who cares about book prizes and literary festivals? My prose might be industrial but my story is beautiful and the only thing that matters but it would be useful if I knew how the bloody thing ends.

CHAPTER SEVENTEEN

It has been a while since I sat in my office. It looks good, considering. No dust has gathered and it is as neat as ever. No one would suspect its lack of productivity.

Deborah sits opposite me and on my pristine desk is yesterday's Daily Mail -the reason for our meeting. I have read it already. Not the paper, just the article, headlined:

Top Breast Surgeon Cheats Death and Lives to Question His Own Survival

To be fair to Rory, he did warn me that the story would run anyway and that he wanted my input, but I did not return his calls or meet with him again. My mistake.

The piece is a full page: twelve hundred words, not the two thousand he said at the outset. It includes a photograph of me from my practice website, a generic photograph of a private jet, an exterior shot of my offices and finally a needless photo of a buxom model who I certainly do not recognise. The sub-headline rankles:

'Medic dubbed 'Dr Boobs' takes a break from his 'celeb' clients to reassess his life after his lucky escape.'

The piece begins rather flatteringly using words and phrases like, 'world renown', 'much sought after' and even 'genius medical student with the profession as his feet', but this is all just a set up for what is to come…

'…a brilliant mind that might have contributed great things to healthcare but instead was seduced by the riches that go with cosmetic surgery…

My previous press coverage is included of course.

'…Doctor Webber is well known for his unacceptable views on women's issues. He has been no-platformed for his misogyny and it is ironic that he has made his millions from the plight of women.'

The plight of women? No-platformed? The bastard. But I have no redress of course. The piece goes on to speculate on the state of my marriage, referencing my extended stay in a 'mid-range and moderately priced London hotel', and concludes that I have been unable to return to work. There is even a suggestion that it might be a sense of guilt which is holding me back. I look across at Deborah and shrug my best, 'so what?', but she is not fooled. Deborah did warn me to stay offline and in particular to avoid any of the comments sections and message boards. Not so easy for a man like me.

Already miserable, I was always going to log on.

The issue with online comments is the lack of any filters. There are no editors and no quality threshold. Everyone is entitled to an opinion, and anonymously too, which only emboldens people. The mob are remote from each other but linked by a keyboard; a virtual kinship, hewn out of hatred.

Deborah was right. I should never have looked. The most common sentiment amongst the bile is people wishing that I had made my flight. In other words, wishing me dead to make the world a better place. Nice. The C word is used frequently; most often as a noun, but occasionally as a verb also. There are helpful suggestions that I should hand over any profits made from my surgery to various women's charities. Others call for me to offer my skills gratis to the thousands of trans people waiting for the surgery that they 'so desperately need.' And no messages whatever of support.

Rory Banks was wrong then. People do not love my story in the way that he promised. Perhaps, it is not so captivating after all, and people certainly do not like me. I didn't care about this before, but I do now because this is the story I am attempting to write and, in the hope, that it will solve everything. How pathetic. My thick skin has evidently thinned with age because I am deeply hurt and now the whole edifice of my life is exposed.

Deborah can't offer much solace either when I explain my literary plans.

"A book?"

"Yes."

""On what?" she asks.

I shrug, feeling embarrassed, "you know. Me. My life."

"What, non-fiction?"

"Err..."

"Like an autobiography?"

I take a moment. Honestly, I am still not clear on this.

"Yeah, I think so."

"Jesus, Gabriel, are you freaking mad?"

I dither again. Yes, perhaps I am.

"And how is it going? The book?"

My look is enough.

"Not great. The tone isn't easy..."

"No, I can see."

I breathe out heavily, "and the ending is..."

"Yes, what is the ending?" she asks directly.

"That's an excellent question. But I'm not sure, which is mainly my reason for writing it."

She looks confused and I don't have the energy to explain. Still beholden to the word count, it has taken me almost thirty-one thousand words to write up to this current moment in my life and reach a complete impasse since I don't know where to take it from here.

"Can I read it?"

"No," I almost laugh.

"Why not? You want people to read it, right?"

The thought of this unnerves me. "Yes, but not yet. It's not ready."

But maybe it is not such a bad idea after all, to get some kind counsel and advice.

"I might be able to help?" she pushes.

"Sure, but let me work on it a little more first."

"Okay then. When?" she asks.

Another good question. I don't know. When I have a blinking ending?

I blame Rory Banks and The Daily Mail but in truth, it is my lack of clarity and poor writing skills that is the cause of my temper tantrum later this afternoon. An expensive lack of control on my part. And painful too.

I stop off at Boots for some much-needed provisions on my return to the Regent Street store. The sales assistant at the Apple Store is not the same person who sold me the machine and this is a good thing. The young woman who appears this time is without tattoos. She does have a very aggressive nose ring though, the sort that pierces the septum leaving the ring to hang, beneath the middle of the nose. It is an odd look, but especially so given her solid and squat build. Dare-I-say-it but bull-like? I sense that she doesn't like me.

The machine is almost brand new and within warranty but I have the receipt with me anyway, which she glances at.

"And you dropped it?" she says, with more than a whiff of glee. This is unnecessary and unhelpful because we both know what really happened. I punched the fucking screen hence my bandaged hand which I know she has clocked, so I don't much care for her tone. She lacks even a scintilla of sympathy and, paranoid, I wonder whether she recognises me from the newspaper article? She doesn't look like a Daily Mail reader but other online publications have picked it up, including The

Guardian, I suspect. She might even be one of my trolls and I shudder. She has that look about her. She has a boyish haircut and a ring on both thumbs which I decide is a sign. Suddenly I am exposed. I feel vulnerable and frightened.

"Can it be fixed now?" I ask hopefully, trying to sound busy.

She stares at her iPad, her dexterous fingers a flurry across the keypad.

"If you leave it with us it can be done by 3pm today. But you will need to pay a deposit."

"Sure, no problem. I can pay now if you like."

"No. Until the engineers look at it they won't know what needs doing. If it's just the screen then-"

"That's fine. Whatever it costs. I don't care."

"Is everything backed up on the machine?"

I pause for a moment which she misinterprets.

"Saved?" Is everything saved Grandad? You misogynist, transphobic old git.

"Yes, it's all saved."

"So, there is nothing important on the mac that could be lost?"

My anxiety is so acute now, I wonder if this is not a veiled criticism of the only document that is on the blinking machine.

"No."

"Nothing important then?" she repeats, not realising how piercing this is.

"Yes, that's right."

"Okay then. All booked in for you."

"Great, thanks man."

Immediately, my eyes widen. Jesus Christ, did I just call her 'man'? I hope for a split second that she hasn't heard me, but her eyes fix me with a glare. It was my silly attempt to be cool and down with the kids, nothing more. Just a clumsy use of language by an old man who is tired of being hated. Until recently, I hardly knew what a pronoun was. Now I do though. I live in fear of the bloody things.

"Sorry about that," I say instinctively, but then stop and the awkwardness continues.

"I wasn't meaning..." I begin and then phase out, unsure how to complete what I have started. I wasn't meaning that you look like a bloke?

She is back on her screen now and I am dismissed.

Sitting in Portman Square again, it is a great relief to be without my laptop. Maybe the machine is at fault and the clever engineers at Apple might be able to flick some switches to show me a way forward. My phone vibrates and I am pleased to see that it is Judy calling, presumably prompted by the article in the newspaper. It has been a long time since we spoke and a good time then to catch up.

"Hi Judy."

"Hi Gabriel. How are you?" she asks in a kindly voice.

"Oh, you know. It's not easy being a celebrity."

"I think the piece is bloody awful. And very unkind."

"Yes, not the best." I don't elaborate that it is doubly painful since it lances my book project on which I have everything pinned. I notice that Judy has a confidence about her now. Over the last three months, she no longer sounds maudlin and has stopped talking about reconciliation. She is also very grateful to me (and with good reason) and I wonder if Stephen might be nibbling at her again, but I don't ask. This vindicates my decision perhaps, but this does not mean that I am not sad.

"Are you still in the same hotel?"

"I am. It's fine for now."

"But it's been so long already. Why don't you find yourself something-"?

"I will, I will. In time. I don't know when."

"And what about your work?"

"What about it?" I ask, worried that she might have a vested interest in my answer.

"Gabriel, it's what you do? I can't imagine what you're doing all day without it?"

A good point. Not writing a book, mainly.

"But you're okay?" she asks again.

"Yes, I will be."

A contradictory answer, which she either misses or decides to ignore.

"Okay then. But you'll call me if I can be a help at all?"

It's an odd thing to say but I am grateful.

"Yes, I will, of course."

"And, Gabriel…"

"Yes?"

"Thank you."

I end the call on these words as a lump instantly forms in my throat.

CHAPTER EIGHTEEN

Now fixed, my laptop is as useless and unhelpful as it was before. I expected as much of course. My book is a complete failing. Dr. Tambor suggests that rekindling my medical career is something that I might consider and that it makes good sense, only it doesn't feel right. In my marrow, I can sense that something is missing; something that will make sense of everything. But I have no idea what and I am tired of waiting. The days have turned into weeks and days go by when I do not even open my tormenting computer. Occasionally, during my walks and encounters, something will occur to me. A phrase or a thought that I might insert somewhere, but it is never anything seismic and nothing that creates any progress.

The Christmas lights on Regent Street seem brighter this year. As a man with no children, the obsession with Santa Claus each December is something I am inured to. Christmas has always been the bonanza season for my medical practice, with ladies wanting to be boob-ready for the festive period and there is also a certain type of man who likes to buy his wife a boob-job for Christmas. My surgery even provides gift vouchers presented in small boxes so that they can be unwrapped on the big day. A present for himself more likely, that he will get to unwrap from March or April onwards.

The meal at Theo Fennels in the Intercontinental Hotel on Park Lane is agreeable enough, even though it signifies that the word is out and that the vultures are circling. I was just grateful to have some company and the excellent food is a bonus. The two gentlemen picking up the bill are investors; speculators who sense an opportunity. Their interest and offer is presented kindly and with no pressure on me to sell. Whichever way I decide to go - to sell my business property in its entirety or just my practice alone - they are interested and, in a position, to move immediately. I thank them and explain my situation without explaining very much at all. Presumably they have seen the Daily Mail article, much like everyone else I have encountered recently. They both hand over their business cards, which I place inside my wallet.

"Thank you both very much for dinner. Really. Most kind."

"Our pleasure. We hope to hear from you. Whenever and however, we can help."

I smile as I leave.

The reception of the hotel is busy and mostly with visitors from the Middle East. If I take a seat and wait, there is a reasonable chance that I might encounter a patient of mine. The door is held open for me by a man wearing a uniform and a hopeful smile. It vanishes when he realises there is nothing about to be pressed into his greedy palm. He doesn't offer to hail me a taxi and who can blame him? Despite the rain, I fancy the walk. It just feels right.

CHAPTER NINETEEN

The labyrinth of subways beneath Hyde Park Corner remain difficult for me to navigate no matter how many times I have used them over the years, and the signs offer little guidance either.

Within these concrete tunnels there are always an array of people asleep atop make-shift cardboard mattresses and some improvised bedding. This evening it is busy, because of the rain I expect. Somehow, seeing people down here seems to be an even harder reality than encountering the homeless above ground and in doorways. I can't really explain why. It just seems so stark and being passed-by by people on their way out somewhere nice and leaving them behind. Or perhaps it's being underground and being closer to their premature graves. Plus, it is a bleak and desolate place, ironically sitting beneath the most expensive real estate on earth. All concrete and always cold, even in the summer with the wind howling through. I wonder what place one needs to occupy in life that this could ever be the best option. In the winter the tunnels are freezing and this evening rain creeps down the stairs and slinks down the ramps to eventually encroach on the improvised beds. A piece of tinsel is stuck onto the tiled wall over one of the births. It looks pathetic.

One of the hotel ballrooms on Park Lane is obviously emptying out as couples head for the London underground. The men look uncomfortable in their tuxedos but not as uncomfortable as the women in their agonising shoes. Another pain borne in the pursuit of beauty. They all hurry past, huddling together now from the homeless instead of the rain, their heads down and in denial at the tragedy before them. And who can blame them? What difference can they make, really? And it might have been a charity ball that they attended, so they've already shelled out and done their bit, right?

I need to be careful now. To my cost, I have chosen poorly in the past and had to endure some very uncomfortable (not to mention one quite dangerous) encounters. A man to my left is asleep, more likely, passed out because in his cup is a collection of coins and a packet of cigarettes which have been left for him. The man directly opposite him is sitting up and watching people as they pass but he is not making any appeals for help. Isn't his plight obvious enough?

He watches me approach. I half smile but he doesn't return the gesture and eyes me carefully. As I arrive, I take a cigarette from my pocket and hand it to him carefully. He will have his own lighter but I am quick to snap open my zippo and offer him a light. He takes the thing willingly and grunts a thank you. In my limited experience, there is no such thing as a homeless person who doesn't smoke. What would be their reasoning? Trying to stay healthy? No doubt it is illegal to smoke in these tunnels, but so too is sleeping I expect and so who cares? His badly chapped and swollen lips pull hungrily on the cigarette.

"Do you mind if I sit down?" I ask tentatively. He doesn't say anything, which is common, and so I settle down. The pungent odour of street life is familiar now as it envelopes me. It can be completely overpowering, as though the person is actually rotting and, in some cases, probably is.

"Hello, my name is Gabriel."

He turns to look at me, his face a study in suspicion.

"I am not a police officer. I don't want anything from you. And I am not going to hurt you in any way."

Since a homeless person came into my life and saved it, I have learnt that the homeless are unable to trust anyone they encounter and especially strangers. He draws heavily on his cigarette, pulling it deeply into his lungs and holding it for as long as he can. Air that is laden with chemicals and toxins but are the least of his concerns. The ground is ice cold, bone hard and painful to sit on. Try it yourself sometime. Sit on the pavement for any length of time with just a wall to lean on; it is painful almost immediately and shortly thereafter, bloody agony.

He remains occupied with his fag as he continues to weigh me up, deciding what my motives might be. Being homeless is a dangerous existence with frequent attacks, assaults and even murders. But he is a big and strong looking man and I imagine he is largely left alone. A frequently broken nose and visible signs of old facial wounds, ex-forces would be my first guess. Finally, he holds up his thumb by way of thanks. With his head still forward, he glances at me for a connection and so I nod and offer him my hand.

"Hi, I'm Gabriel."

After a moment, he takes my hand and we shake. His hand is enormous and dwarfs mine. It is ice cold and hard, swollen with the cold. I can feel his many calluses beneath the dark veneer of dirt and street grime that has been layered over time. Given my hygiene neurosis, it is progress that I can shake his hand at all, and I feel ashamed of the man I was when I met Catherine.

"I'm Troy," he says finally. He sounds exhausted.

"Nice to meet you, Troy."

He laughs. "Is it?"

His cigarette burns angrily as his lungs pull the flame closer to his fattened and injured mouth. A fall or a punch?

I have been doing this for a few months now; engineering encounters and speaking with people on the streets. A little over four months to be exact. It began in the hope that someone would know Catherine and help me to find her. This hope quickly faded but I carried on anyway as part of my proactive phase – making things happen, hoping to force the issue and find answers and closure. Nothing happened of course and yet I continue with them because I have come to enjoy their company. Or most of them, anyway. And much better than speaking with no one.

I am interested in their lives also and I enjoy the feeling that comes with being able to help. Another elegant looking couple walk past. Water is cascading from the man's umbrella which he is holding at knee height. He glances down at me and looks a little confused at the odd couple before him, which is understandable.

"Will you get moved on from here?" I ask, half interested but more to show him that I know something of his world and in doing so, gain his trust. Everything here hinges on trust.

"Yeah, sometimes. But not tonight. Not when it's pissing down."

I don't know whether this is dispensation by the officials or because they don't fancy getting wet themselves. The latter I expect. I offer him another cigarette which he lights himself using his old fag. The smoking ban is now so absolute, it is rare to smell tobacco nowadays. His new cigarette burns brightly, which is attractive against the gloom and even more so as a tiny heat source. Troy cups the tiny flame within his hand to trap the heat between frequent drags.

"Do you mind if I join you?"

He looks bemused since I am sitting next to him already, but what I mean is in sharing a cigarette with him. I pop one into my mouth and shift my numb bottom as I do because it is already aching in protest and my troublesome right knee is making its presence felt also.

He smiles and holds up his cigarette as a lighter, which I lean across to meet.

This is a new departure for me. If Deborah or Judy could see me now they would simply not believe their eyes. I have never smoked a cigarette before in my life. Not one. Not even a puff in my youth when practically the entire school was pretending to be addicted. I splutter a little as my cigarette takes light. He watches me closely as I suck hard on the foam filter and inhale deeply. And then, lights out.

Instantly my head clouds and forces my eyes shut as a wave of nausea completely envelopes me. As I exhale, barely conscious, I begin to cough and splutter, the smoke escaping haphazardly. No smoke rings and neat plumes from me. My head feels so light, I feel overwhelmingly tired and a need to sleep. My head is so heavy. Too heavy to hold up and I can feel my torso slipping down against the rough concrete wall. I feel a hand grabbing my sleeve to ease my descent and I hear some distant laughter too. On the ground now, I lie still and feel oddly comfortable, although my stomach grumbles and threatens to reproduce my expensive meal. I don't know how long I remain like this. A few minutes maybe? Eventually, my breathing shallows and my head starts to clear. I open my eyes and take in my odd view. I must have fainted.

I remain comfortable even on the harsh concrete floor, as though I am in bed in one of the plush hotels above us. I hear the noise of pedestrians hurrying by and then more laughter. My head continues to clear and as it does, the pains in my bottom and legs begin to re-emerge. As I try to right myself, I can feel Troy's heavy paw pulling me upright and his laughter again which is now almost hysterical. Fully upright again, I stare at the opposite wall and wait for my brain to fully engage.

"Jesus Christ," I splutter, which Troy finds even more hilarious. He grabs my box of cigarettes from me, studies the box and then whoops again.

"Silk Cut. They're only fucking Silk Cut."

Even I know that these are a mild cigarette and so my shame is compounded. I can't take my tobacco. Okay, guilty as charged. Troy finishes off yet another cigarette (with no such ill-effects) and I can see the funny side as well now. So, we both laugh hard, egging each other on. We must make an unlikely sight for passers-by, two homeless people guffawing in delight and having more fun than anyone around them.

"You don't smoke then?" Troy suggests.

"No. Can you tell?" I reply, which sets him off again.

"It was like you did brown."

I have learnt that Brown is 'street' for heroin.

"No, I would draw the line at heroin."

Troy shrieks in delight. "Quite right. It'd kill you stone dead. Plus, I wouldn't give you any of my brown if I had some anyway."

"No. Good. That is good to know, thanks."

Such encounters are usually much more tentative, with cagey openings where I am mindful not to pry. But this one has tobacco as an accelerant and Troy's defences are almost completely obliterated.

"Fuck me, man. I can't remember the last time I've laughed like that."

Laughter is said to be the best medicine and there is some truth to this. It floods our nervous system with endorphins which suppress stress hormones, and so doing, can alleviate pain. In this instance then, cigarettes are medicinal and a force for good.

I hand Troy my lit cigarette and he takes it gratefully. My smoking career is over after a solitary puff. My head is completely clear now and with this, I need to shuffle my bottom once again. Troy remains statue still, inured to any discomfort.

"Thanks for stopping man. You've really cheered me up."

"My pleasure," I reply, and I mean it, but it is too complicated to explain. I wonder about his background. Army? Broken home? A violent dad? No dad at all? A low-income family? Uneducated? Broken marriage? Jail time? Sherlock Holmes would not be stretched here.

"Why did you stop?" Troy asks. By now, I really should have a satisfactory answer for this, but I don't.

"It's a long story. As long as yours I suspect."

Troy smiles. His teeth are completely ruined and would probably would not survive a single toffee. I put him at late thirties and his chances of reaching my age at nil, if he remains on the streets that is. I suppose pneumonia will be the most likely cause of his demise.

"I'm glad you did though, thanks."

"I'm glad too," I reply. "How long has it been?"

"What, like this, homeless?"

He coughs heavily.

"On and off, five years. Since discharge. I were a para."

I know my military history well enough; The Parachute Regiment, one of the most elite army units in the world, with a motto: Ready for Anything. How poignant for Troy now. "How many tours?"

"Five."

Five. I feel humbled. Troy too, is lucky to be alive.

"Sierra Leone, Kosovo, Iraq and Afghanistan. Twice."

He doesn't say how he came to leave and I don't ask. Never pry.

"And what about you? What's your story?"

I breathe out and make a quick assessment. "We are worlds apart, you and I. A different route, but not such a different endpoint."

Troy looks at me oddly.

"Because in a different way, I'm lost too."

Troy chuckles.

"Yeah, well, some of us are more lost than others."

Instantly, I feel silly for making the comparison and I have a need to apologise, which perhaps he senses because he heads me off.

"No, I get it." He begins. "You mean we all struggle, right?"

"Yeah, I guess. But like you say, some more than others."

At this he nods and I smile, relieved.

"So, the army then?" I ask, changing the subject.

"Yeah, I loved it. Bloody loved it. Every minute."

I detect an accent now. Yorkshire, maybe? Northern anyway.

"Truth be told, it saved my life." He continues.

I've heard this before.

"No question. Without the army, I wouldn't be here. Ironic

that, eh?"

"Yeah and five tours?"

"An IED in Afghanistan - lost half my stomach."

Immediately, I imagine the field surgeons who kept him alive. I feel a sense of shame.

"The way I'm made, getting paid to fight was perfect for me."

"And the opposite for me. Not much of a fighter, me."

"No, well, you sound clever. You don't need to fight."

This stops me for a moment.

"And what about now then?" I ask tentatively. "Still fighting?"

Troy lights another cigarette. He has the packet now. He sucks in the smoke and screws his face up as he thinks about my question.

"Yeah, always fighting but there's nothing for me anymore. Not now."

I don't say anything.

"Lads like me… when they come out they go in to security, you know, stuff like that…"

I gesture enquiringly.

"But you have to be clean."

I don't say anything. No need to and he sniffs heavily, as though confirming his dependency.

"Plus, I've done some time, you know?"

He keeps saying 'you know', only I don't. I have no concept of his life at all.

"And I don't blame them either." He continues.

"No?" I ask kindly.

'No. Not really. I wouldn't give me a chance. When me mam died, I couldn't be on me own with her."

I shake my head, confused.

"In her house when she were lying in her coffin? I couldn't be left there alone cos I'd have nicked the rings off her fingers."

I shake my head.

"Christ. That's awful."

"Yeah, it is. But that's how it is on the gear. It's all you can think about."

Despite his words and cruel reality, he has a sense of dignity still, instilled no doubt by his elite regiment. That he was selected for the regiment and served for so long is a testament to his character, and the reason why it is so sad that he is now so broken.

"And what about your buddies?" I ask.

He shrugs sadly. "Yeah, some left, you know? But a lot of them have gone, either in the field or since."

I nod, unsure what I might add.

"A lot of em have offed themselves which is super sad."

Again, nothing from m, not even that I've thought of it myself.

"I've been close myself, you know."

I just shrug.

"But you haven't," I say finally.

"Nah, still fighting, eh?" he barks proudly!

Some of the lads did okay, though. The officers mainly, you know? But they're different, like, you know? They come from a different place to us.

Like me is what he means.

"You know, clever. Been to school and university, like you I bet."

I smile and take the hit, if this is what it is.

"They also have families, you know? They've got people. Or people who can help. That's the real difference."

These are my problems revealed, but I am careful now not to draw anymore parallels between us. The centenary of The Great War has just passed and with much being made of our servicemen, their sacrifices and their on-going battles.

"And what about the charities?" I ask.

"Yeah. They're good. Yeah. Excellent people and they do what they can."

An answer which also begs the question… so why are you trying to sleep in a tunnel?

"Right, and?"

He sighs as he contemplates this.

"Yeah, I can go to them. But they have records, you know? And it's difficult, you know? You really need to be clean if you want help."

A vicious circle that does not need explaining.

"And what drugs are you on?"

He laughs at this.

"Anything I can get. I'm not choosey, me, but hopefully something stronger than Silk Cut!"

Again, we both laugh. I have five more boxes in my coat pocket which I will hand over shortly.

"But what can I do?" he asks. "Just stop?"

I nod in agreement, although I rage at the notion of drug abuse being called a disease.

"And your people then? Any family?" I ask warily. He takes a moment and I sense his pain. I am about to change the subject when he starts up again.

"Yeah, wife. Two kids. Boy and a girl. Kylie and Troy Junior. Meant the world to me…" He shakes his head. "But I didn't do right by em." He fidgets now and begins to pull at his face.

"I hurt them. And Karen, my wife… I can't blame her. I don't, not anymore anyway. I know that now. She did it to protect 'em. It's what I should have done, I can see that now."

He pops the cigarette into his mouth and uses his swollen fingers to massage his eyes.

"I'm sure you did your best."

"No… not by a long chalk. I caught her with 'im."

I wince, imagining an aggrieved Para.

"I thought he were just some bloke, you know?"

I don't pry any further.

"But they're still together. Married now."

"Oh."

"So, he were someone she loved. Not just some bloke what I nearly killed… he's their dad now too." Troy sobs gently now.

"I'm sure you didn't mean to hurt him?"

He looks at me oddly.

"I fockin did. I put him in a chair for the rest of his life."

I shudder. I can't imagine the pain it must have caused for them all, and the guilt.

I need to adjust my legs as a searing pain breaks through the numbness and I almost shriek. Troy has still not moved.

"What now then?" I ask.

He shrugs. "Just day to day, you know. Getting through each day. Some good, mostly bad. But today's good - since you rocked up anyway."

"Thanks Troy. That's kind of you to say that. Thanks."

"And what about you?"

"What do you mean?"

"You said you were lost?"

"Oh, yes. Well, in my way, I am.'

"Yeah, I get that. I know what you mean. Everything's relevant, right?"

"Err…"

"You got a family?"

"No. A wife, but no kids. And we're separated."

"Oh, that's tough."

"Yeah. Nice to have people, as you say."

"It's not just having people," he states.

"What do you mean?"

"It's having people who need you. That's it. You know, being needed."

I ponder this moment of wisdom.

"Yes, I can see that."

"People who need you and you're responsible for, that's very important."

"Yeah, well, I think it's a bit late for me now,' I add mournfully.

He turns and looks at me carefully.

"Hey… don't be too hard on yourself."

I smile. "No?"

"No. You mark my words. I think you'll be fine."

I don't say anything. I just nod.

"Yeah. I know it. I might only have half me guts but I still get feelings in them. And I've a good feeling about you."

"Well, thanks, because that is good to know."

My legs are in agony now and I need to get off the freezing floor. From the look of the pedestrians, the rain has stopped, which makes it a good time to take my leave.

I stand up and immediately blood urgently rushes into my previously restricted veins, accompanied by pain as I begin fumbling in my coat pockets. I produce my batch of cigarettes and his face falls a little flat.

"You said, you weren't choosey." I joke.

He smiles and shakes his head, almost as an apology.

"What is it?" I ask.

"Nah, it's nothing. It's silly. Sorry."

But I can sense something is wrong and I am intrigued.

"No, go on. What is it?"

He looks a little bashful now. "I just thought you might be someone else, that's all."

"What do you mean? Who?"

He shakes his head again. "Nah, don't worry about it. I don't mean to sound ungrateful. You've been great."

"No, Troy, please, its important. Who did you think I was?"

He considers me for a moment and then sighs.

"There's this bloke going around, we call him the Fifty Guy…"

My heart leaps at this.

"…and I hoped that it might be you. But, please, just forget it."

I stare in disbelief.

"The Fifty Guy?"

Quickly I sit back down again and place the cigarettes in his lap.

"The Fifty Guy?"

"Yeah. Well, that's what we call him anyway."

"Why?"

He takes a moment.

"Because he gives out fifty-pound notes to homeless

people, brand new ones as well."

I know exactly how many fifty-pound notes that I have dispensed. I know where and when because each is noted in my diary. Seventy-two to date, a little over three and half grand. A pittance to me, but worth every penny to see the delight on the recipient's faces. Just like I did with Catherine, I wonder what they spend it on and whether I am being kind or naïve and misguided. But the way the tobacco eased my senses earlier on, who can blame them if it keeps their painful reality at bay?

I like the idea that I have a name and that people are speaking about me in a positive light. It is a welcome departure from the online hate mobs - so organised and determined - or the Bridge clubs in Maurice's synagogue, laughing at the greedy squirrel. But what excites me also is the sense of a community that Troy belongs to - a club that no one wants to join but nevertheless, it is people bound together by their circumstances. Immediately I think of Catherine, because if there is such a community then presumably there will be someone who knows of her and will know how to find her?

"Troy, if I were looking for someone…"

"Who?"

"Someone who is homeless… how would I go about it?"

Troy stares at me, his mind racing as something is occurring to him. Suddenly he adopts a more knowing look.

"A young woman? You're looking for a young woman?"

I smile my agreement.

"Jesus, it is you."

I nod now.

"It is you. You're the Fifty Guy."

"I am."

"I knew it! I knew there was something about you."

"Can you help me find her?" I continue, but his face lengthens again and he shakes his head. "Not so easy. People come and go on the streets. It's a big place if you want to get lost and some people don't want to be found."

"No, I've tried the hostels."

"Women especially, cos they've got more places to go. More options. Did she have a kid?"

"No."

He tuts. "Maybe impossible then. Who is she anyway? A girlfriend?"

"No, she could be my daughter. Her name is Catherine," I sigh at the number times I have recounted this tale and how hopeless I sound. "I met her on the street, just off Old Bond Street."

"What, like how we met?" He asks.

"No, no exactly."

"But you gave her money? Fifty quid?"

Immediately I blush as I think back to our encounter. And then I nod because it is easier than explaining.

"Well, then, you made her day. But I can't help you find her, sorry."

"No, don't worry. But thank you anyway."

Ahead two men enter the subway. Orthodox Jews. They are both tall and thin, accentuated by their long black coats, beards and tall black hats. A unique look. For all the obvious talents of the Jewish people, fashion design is not amongst them (although Calvin Klein, Ralph Lauren, Donna Karan and many others will disagree I am sure). I watch them carefully. As they draw level with us their hands remain in their pockets, their eyes fixed forward. Troy grimaces as they pass.

"Never had a penny from that lot," Troy spits and I manage not to react. But he is not finished yet.

"Only ever help themselves, them lot."

I smile at his political incorrectness.

"What?" Troy demands to know.

I shake my head and watch as comprehension dawns on him.

"Ah, shit. You're not one of them, are you?"

"One of them?" I splutter.

"What is it? Amish? I seen that film years ago with that bloke… Hans Solo."

"They're not Amish," I correct him but I don't bother with

Mr. Ford and his hurt feelings.

"No?" Troy asks.

"No, they're Jewish."

"Right, and is that what you are?" He asks fearfully, probably thinking of the crisp red note he might now forego.

"No. I'm not."

"Oh, thank fuck for that."

"But my wife is."

"Ah, shit, she's not?"

I chuckle as I nod my head.

"Fuck, man, I am so sorry. I swear…"

"No, don't worry. The last time I encountered an orthodox Jew I wanted to kill him."

This stops Troy.

"Why? What did he do?"

I shake my head.

"Hey, you don't have any mates do you, who do that kind of thing?" I ask to deflect his attention and relieve any awkwardness.

"Yeah, I do actually."

"Good. Then I might need them yet."

Troy chuckles.

"And what does she wear?"

'Who?"

"Your wife. Does she wear this crazy stuff too?"

I shriek with laughter at this.

"No, she's not religious."

"Oh, only it's not a great look. They must love their God to wear that get up."

More laughter from us both.

"Oh, come off it, those ringlets with the hair? What's all that about?"

"I think that's the whole point."

"What do you mean?'

"They don't care what they look like, as long as it pleases their God."

"And does it?" Troy asks incredulously.

"Who knows, I'm not Jewish."

Troy considers this. He looks pensive and then nods.

"Ah, well. That's a shame for me and you both then.'

This surprises me. "Really?"

"Yeah. You know?"

No, I don't. "How do you mean?"

"You know, having a God."

I don't reply.

"I envy people that."

"Really"

"Yeah. You know, because it must be nice to have a God. To think there's something out there, looking out for you."

I ponder this for a moment.

"Is it something you get taught or do you think you get born with it?" Troy asks.

"Err…" These are big questions.

"And it must be nice having something to believe in, you know? I used to have the army but then they got rid of me. Been downhill ever since. Do you reckon God would do that, chuck you out like that?"

I sigh. "I don't know, I guess not."

"But those lads… the ones with the hats, they must be on to something?"

"How do you mean?"

"Well they're rich, aren't they? Those Jewish lads?"

Yet more laughter from us both.

"Not all of them are, no."

"But a lot of them?" Troy insists.

"Some of them, certainly, yes."

"Like you then?" he asks, blunt as you like.

"Err…"

"Well you are the Fifty Guy, right? So, you aint poor."

He isn't being rude and he is right, of course. I am rich and my wealth entirely defines me. Or at least it did. I have not felt wealthy since my encounter with Catherine.

Troy is waiting for my answer.

"That depends on what you're measuring by…"

He laughs hard at this.

"Because if wealth is measured in friendships or family…"

"Do you have loads of money?" Troy cuts to the point.

"Yes. That I do have."

"Then you're rich and you should thank God every day."

"Right."

This is a curious proposition since God has nothing to do with my success or my daily life. It was down to plain hard work and a brilliant mind. But then, isn't my great mind a gift? And if so, from whom?

"Seriously, man, thank him."

"But I don't have a God."

"Then get one."

"What?"

"I would."

"Then why don't you?" I go back with and not unreasonably.

"Because what would I thank him for?" Troy asks. Fair point.

"But he could look out for you?" I suggest.

This stops him for a moment and he shrugs.

"Yeah, I spose. And how come you've got no friends, anyway?"

It's a good question and one I don't wish to answer.

"Long story."

"Right, well, I'm not going anywhere. I've got all night."

I let out a timely chuckle as I pass off my wet eyes as laughter and I get up off the floor for the second time. I can feel that my trousers are wet and I have a good idea that it is not rain, but I don't mind. Troy starts to get up also.

"No, don't get up."

"Shut up man. If I don't get up then how can I hug you?"

I smile broadly, as happy as I am sad. He is tall, much taller than me as he wraps his arms around me and we hug. My face presses into his matted beard.

"Thank you, Troy," I whisper as I press a stack of crisp notes into his hand, just as I had done with Catherine. He looks down at me and nods. I have no doubt that Troy will use the money to get loaded, but who am I to judge him?

He nods at me. "Thank you, Gabriel. Just like me, man. Don't give up, eh."

"Thanks, I won't."

As I get to the ramp, I turn around. Troy has a new cigarette in his mouth and stares after me with the broadest smile on his face. Quickly, he stands to attention and salutes, the way he would have done to his commanding officers on his many tours. I am crying openly now, sure that he can't see my tears. I am happy for him, but desperately sad for myself.

The rain continues to pour. There are taxis passing but I ignore them. I am already wet and I want to be alone. I walk up Park Lane, a street made famous by a board game. Owning a Park Lane property might win Monopoly but that doesn't always translate in the real world. I am a testament to this. In the houses and apartments to my right are the world's richest people, but they are people with problems just like everyone else. Everything is relevant, as Troy would say.

CHAPTER TWENTY

Back in my hotel room I take a long, hot shower and feel a pang of guilt. Firstly, at my pleasure to wash Troy's pungent smell from my skin, but more because I imagine how much he would love a shower himself and a warm towel. The rain crashes hard against my window as I draw the blinds and I think of him outside. 'Everything is relevant?' I smile at his array of endearing quirks.

I have no intentions of going to bed. As well as Troy, I think of Catherine and the other people I have met on the streets. Flicking through my notebook, I look at their names, where I met them and any observations that I have jotted down. One man, just along from Kings Cross, was unable to even give me his name. I think of him now and what he might be doing. Is he even still alive? I hope that he is and that he is somewhere dry on this filthy night.

I open my laptop for the first time in three weeks and scroll through my 'masterpiece' to the end, where the 'hero' of the story is holed up in a hotel, all alone and with writer's block.

Now though, at least, I have something to write. I can force the issue and make things happen because the connection I made with Troy tonight somehow feels relevant. Perhaps I am clutching but I sense that it has a meaning and this buoys me.

The laughter we shared, our mutual failings, and the connection that comes when two men hug each other whilst both of us are crying.

I order coffee from room service and quickly get to work chronicling my evening, hoping for meaning. The signs are encouraging because my writing is more fluent. The words come easily and I finish the chapter in a flurry.

It is 2 am when I scroll back through my work: surprisingly good by my own low standards. A gust of wind bashes rain hard against my window and I think of Catherine again. I wonder where she is and whether she is alright. Looking back at my computer, I come to the section I have written about the two Orthodox Jews who Troy was so disparaging of.

…unmissable in their unique outfits. Troy regards them with an inkling of a sneer. Blatant racism and yet I don't rebuke him. Mindful not to judge but Troy's length of transgressions continues then: vagrancy, smoking in a non-smoking area, paralysing his ex-wife's future husband, drug use and finally the most heinous crime of all, causing offence. Ridiculous of course, because he doesn't offend me, not really - and I've even got used to his body odour, which is far more offensive than anything he says. I try to recall his exact words. They made me laugh at the time. Something like, 'never had a penny out of this lot.'

So much meat on the bone here, just where would the mob start? Playing to the stereotype that Jews are mean, even if he does think they're Amish. And the use of the pejorative 'this lot' is damning too; up there with 'you people', which can ruin a career these days. The court of public opinion finds you guilty, which achieves nothing unless sanctimony is valued. And it doesn't matter if Troy happens to be telling the truth; that no orthodox Jews have ever stopped to give him any money, for this might be the case. No matter. Guilty as charged.

I read the passage again and chuckle at my irreverence. I imagine the mob, frothing with indignation if they were ever to read it. Surely such a book would be burned, or at least banned. I continue on…

It so happens that Jewish people are not mean as the stereotype suggests. In fact, considerable tithes are realized by synagogues and a great many Jews are prominent philanthropists, such as Arnold Weinstock,

Jack Lyons and Guy de Rothschild; each giving up many billions of dollars to worthy causes.

I read until the end and retire to bed with a sharp pang of sadness. I have not had any flashes of inspiration as I had hoped for. I lie awake, unable to sleep. I think of the two Jewish men and I feel guilty at the fun that Troy and I had at their expense. Not that they would care; they are well used to the odd looks and sniggers and must now be immune. It probably even emboldens them, that they have such faith and convictions. It is a sad reality that Jews are so maligned but they are not to be pitied. It is highly likely that these two men are successful: professionals, almost certainly; highly educated; married with children and part of a large and fiercely loyal community. Certainly, more complete then me as I lie in my bed, unable to sleep for the doubts and fear that have returned to torment me.

CHAPTER TWENTY-ONE

In the morning I wake a little later than normal, although it feels as though I have not slept at all. Not even another hot shower can revive me. I did not drink any alcohol yesterday and yet I feel heavily hungover, or have just flown in from Australia. My eyes are heavy and my head hurts, but at least I have some clarity now as to how to proceed even if it feels a little ethereal and desperate.

It is a little before 7am and so too early to make contact then? I wonder if I should call or send a text? I certainly cannot just show up, unannounced. I must give some warning for it would be rude not to and possibly even compromising. This is all new territory for me, but at least I have arrived at a plan. A long shot at best.

I open my laptop and read the last chapter again. It is not as good as I remember and certainly not as good as the experience of meeting Troy; my writing deficiencies exposed once again. If ever I do complete this story I might need to have it rewritten for me. I make some edits and add a sentence or two. I re-read the paragraphs about the Orthodox Jews, which on reflection, I decide are unnecessary and so I delete them. I sigh noisily. This bloody book.

I wait until the 8 am news bulletin is over and then I send

my text. Easier than phoning, just in case she is not alone. Russell has been keeping me informed and it seems that Judy is quickly adjusting to her new life.

Hi, it's me. If you're about today, I wonder if I could pop over? Whatever time suits you.

As it is with modern communications, as soon as I hit the send button I feel vulnerable waiting for a reply. Fifteen anxious minutes pass. Perhaps she is in the shower, or maybe ushering a new lover from my house. My phone pings.

Sure, it will be lovely to see you. 10am?

I walk around Hyde Park nervously for an hour to clarify my thoughts and rehearse what I might say. Not much clarity comes, which is no surprise. However, I frame it, Judy will be astounded. But I am sure she will be pleased and even happy. And then, of course, I fret.

My house looks as handsome as ever as I approach on foot from Dorset Street. Across the road I notice a new French restaurant has opened and I wonder if Judy has visited yet? I expect she has. With whom, I wonder? I have a key but out of politeness I ring the bell at a little after 10am, as we agreed. As I wait, I am nervous and pull my hand through my thinning hair. I have lost weight and I wonder if she will notice. The door opens and Judy smiles broadly. She too has lost weight which I notice immediately, and something which becomes even more apparent as we hug each other affectionately. New perfume as well?

"You look well," I say.

"Thank you. It's good to see you. How have you been?"

"Oh, you know."

She nods. She knows exactly and is kind enough not to probe. I note that she has not said that I look well.

"You're still at the hotel?"

"Yeah well, you know me."

We go through to the kitchen. The heart of any house, it is warm and comforting with its gleaming range and underfloor heating. Judy fills a teapot from the hot tap and takes a box of expensive Florentines from the larder. She empties them onto a china plate.

We sit opposite each other at the bar and her demeanour changes. A sense of anxiety comes over her now and I can guess why. She pours our tea.

"I've been worried about you."

I smile. "No need to, Judith. Don't worry, I haven't changed my mind."

I'm aware as I say it that my choice of language is a little self-pitying, and possibly cruel.

"Sorry, I didn't mean it like that," I add quickly.

"I know," she smiles.

"Just that… I know it's what's best for us."

She nods in agreement. Her relief is palpable and she smiles. We could have continued as a couple, I am sure of it. Laboured on without ever knowing how miserable we were. She reaches for my hands and we squeeze each other.

"Deborah has been keeping me up to date."

"Ah, of course."

"Gabriel, what can I do to help?"

I breathe in heavily and exhale slowly. Where to begin? I think back to my earlier rehearsals in Hyde Park.

"You need to get back to work. It's what you do."

I sigh.

"Deborah would love it. You and her working again."

As would Judith with her bonanza divorce settlement - including half my future earnings - but I don't say this. Judith has my interests at heart here. I think or I hope.

"Since the accident, I've been doing a lot of thinking…"

She nods and waits. "And I've discovered some things about myself. Stuff I never realised before. You know, some good, some not so good."

"Okay, then let's start with the positive."

"Oh right… Erm…"

Judith tuts impatiently.

"Bloody hell, you haven't changed."

"Oh, no, I have. I have definitely changed."

"Then come on, the good things?"

"Okay, that I can be kind."

A look of surprise takes hold, which is rather unhelpful.

"That I enjoy being generous."

"Oh, I see." She looks bashful now.

"I don't mean our settlement. Which is…"

"Very bloody kind of you."

"Thank you, but no less than you deserve."

She needs a moment at this.

"It's more than you needed to concede."

I think of Russell and I half smile. I shrug.

"I've realised some of my follies also," I add, keen to get away from my positives and to the reason for my visit.

"Hang on, so that's it with the good stuff?"

I chuckle at this. She always had a good sense of humour.

"Did Deborah mention to you anything about the woman I'm looking for?"

Judith looks a little pitying now.

"She did I'm afraid. She doesn't understand it."

"No. Well, nor do I, so that makes two of us."

"Someone you met on the streets?" Judith states.

"Yes, pretty much."

"But how? You don't stop for homeless people?"

I smile again.

"The thing is…" I begin, recalling the imaginary lines from my walk earlier.

"Yes, go on," Judy says, intrigued now.

"I'm not the great success story I've always thought I was."

"No?" Judith gestures with her hands to our beautiful kitchen as if to contradict me.

"No. I don't mean as a surgeon, or as a professional success. I don't mean income-wise. I mean as a person."

"Oh, I see."

"And maybe it's because of my work and my obsession with it. I've always been so manic about making money, I never stopped to realise just how lonely I am. And how empty I feel."

This is a lot for Judith to take in. It could be an oblique

criticism of her and must be hurtful for her to hear.

"But isn't that because you love your work..."

"Which is my point. I don't love my work, I just love the wealth it provides."

"Right, but-"

"Because money has become the only thing I really love. The trappings of wealth... 'trapped' is a good word actually because that's how I feel.'

This is a line I had worked out beforehand; not quite delivered as I had hoped, but effective enough.

"How much do I have? How much more? How can I spend it before it's too late? My home, my bank balances, my jewellery, your jewellery..."

This is not comfortable listening for Judith but her ears do prick up at the mention of my jewellery. 'What jewellery?' might be her reasonable response. Luckily, I am able to pass it off as an error and move her on.

"So how generous am I, really?"

Judith looks awkward now.

"Well, we all like to feather our nests. Who doesn't?" she says defensively, in her ten-million-pound home.

I shake my head. "I sound so hackneyed I know, but money is not what life should be about."

"Of course! But Gabriel, you have so much else besides."

"Really? Like what?" I ask, perhaps unkindly.

"Well, we've got friends..." she pleads, but realises how hollow this sounds as I shake my head. She goes quiet.

"This is going to surprise you," I say.

She girds herself. "Go on. What is it?"

"Do you think there is a Rabbi I might speak with?"

Judith's eyes pop. Not that she is so religious but her Judaism has always had a bearing on our marriage and at times has been contentious. Her social life is heavily immersed in Jewish life and something that I have always felt detached from.

"Well, that is a surprise."

I sigh.

"You don't want to convert, do you?"

"I don't know what I want. I just need some help. Some guidance. Can you arrange it for me?"

Judith continues to stare at me, shocked, but I can tell her mind is whirring.

"Well, there's Ruth Biel. She's very approachable and young and full of energy."

I shake my head. I am not so good with young people.

"You'd prefer a man?"

And there's that too. I am grateful to Judith for not making me say it.

"There's Rabbi Greenstein, Sol Greenstein that I also know."

"He sounds very Jewish."

"Oh, he is. And he's old. Seen everything already."

"Good. Then maybe, Sol is the man. If you could make an introduction for me."

CHAPTER TWENTY-TWO

Two days later, I am punctual for my meeting at 11am with Rabbi Greenstein. His house is a modest maisonette in Stanmore from where he has somehow reared five children, all of whom have left home now. We sit in his grubby kitchen and I try to imagine how much food this tiny space has provided over the years.

Sol is in his late sixties. A small man with a straggly beard, he places my tea in front of me and says a quick prayer for us both.

"So, your wife tells me that you are lost?"

"Yes, you could say that."

"But you found here okay?"

I laugh.

"So, not so lost then?" he chirps and I laugh again.

"I guess."

"Did you get a ticket for your car?"

"No, I took a taxi actually."

"Good. That's smart. Probably cheaper too with these bastards on their mopeds giving out tickets like confetti. It's just another tax."

I smile.

"What are the roads like? Busy with Christmas?"

"Not really, not that I noticed anyway. Pretty good. Half an hour maybe from Marylebone?"

"People are buying stuff online now."

"Yes, that seems to be the way these days. It's the future of shopping.'

"Pah. I don't agree. Everyone inside, no one talking."

I nod. Even if I disagreed with Rabbi Greenstein, I would nod.

"You take a taxi or do you use Uber?"

"No, black taxi. Old school."

"Good. I don't like Uber. Everything's an app these days. And they call it progress? I don't think so."

On the wall are a series of family photographs, the various graduation shots being the most prominent. I like him immediately. His intelligence is obvious and his irascible nature is irresistible.

"So, why are you here?" he asks gruffly.

"Err…"

"Why a rabbi? You're not a Jew?"

"No. I'm a Christian. But lapsed."

"Okay then, so why me? Why not, a priest?"

I might have been prepared to answer this. But I am not and I shake my head.

The truth is that I have reached the end of the road and I am desperate. But I suspect Sol will not enjoy being a last resort and so I just shrug. I could explain that I have a feeling; an instinct about fate and that this is where I feel I should be, but I don't.

"So, what can I do for you? I have just one hour."

"Oh-"

"If we need more then we can reschedule. If I can help, that is. I get the feeling that I might be a last resort."

I smile and, for the first time, Sol does too.

I have had two days to prepare for this meeting and so I am almost fluent as I recount my whole story. Sol listens intently and says little, his eyebrows doing the talking for him. When I am finished, he slurps at his tepid tea and pulls at his beard.

"That's quite a story."

"Thank you."

"It would make a good book."

I laugh loudly at this.

"And you survived."

"Here I am."

"Which is a good thing. And you want to know why."

"Yes, I do. Amongst other things."

"I think you know already."

"No, I have no idea. That's why I'm here," I protest.

"But you think I might know?"

"Yes, I hope."

"No, I don't. I have no idea."

He doesn't soften at all, he is as blunt as a butter knife. There is no grey or nuance with Sol, which is pretty crushing.

"Why? You think this is a God thing?" he asks brusquely, and with an accusatory tone that implies I might have a self-importance issue.

"I don't know. I don't know what this is. That's why I'm here, baring my soul to you, because I am desperate to know."

"Yeah, well, get over yourself. We're all desperate to a point, right?"

I don't know how to respond to this. Sol is not the shoulder I had been hoping for and I am becoming cross with Judith for sending me to him.

"What are your thoughts?" he asks. "What's your hunch?"

"Well…" I begin, tentative now. "I'm not religious, as you know, but somehow this feels fated."

"But that doesn't mean by God."

"Oh?"

I wait for his further explanation but nothing comes.

"Then by who?"

But he shrugs, "how should I know?"

"Well…"

"Sometimes things just happen and we don't know why."

I nod but this is not helping very much. Not helping at all and I've hit another bloody dead end.

"Maybe you are solely responsible for it?" he suggests.

"Me, how so?"

"I don't know."

Jesus Christ. Aren't you meant to be the wise one, here?

"Then what do you know?" I ask.

"Hey," Sol snaps. "I just know what I know. That's it."

"Sure, but-"

"This could just be you seeing the error of your ways with the money and the jewels."

"Sure, but the plane crash and the food poisoning?"

He gestures with his hand. "Yep, that is definitely odd."

"Right, and so I don't know what to do. I feel lost. Sometimes I feel like I have died - as though I did make my flight."

"But you didn't. You missed it."

"Yes-"

"So, you feel that you've been given a pass."

"Yes, I guess."

"And you don't want to waste it?"

"Right, but unless I can understand why, how can I figure out what to do?"

Sol mulls on this for a moment, chewing his lips and pulling at his beard.

"Because I don't think that I have been spared so I can continue on with my old life."

Sol seems to agree with this and nods.

"Which means that my old self is dead, metaphorically at least."

Sol nods again. "Assuming there is a reason," he says, finally, "and not just your good fortune."

"There is. There is a reason. I know it. I can feel it. It happened for a reason. But I don't know what it is."

"More tea?"

"No, thank you."

I like him less now. The kettle re-boils and he pours himself a refill, probably out of boredom more than thirst.

"You sure?" he asks, eyeing the kettle.

"Positive."

It has been helpful to offload my story but not so enlightening. No epiphany, anyway.

"I don't believe that this is the work of a God," I begin, thinking out loud.

Sol slurps his new cup of tea.

"You know, that he's up there, pulling strings and making things happen like this," I explain.

"But you do believe that it was fate?"

"Yes, I think I do."

"So, you have been chosen then?"

"Yes. That's how I feel, which is a contradiction I know. But my life is full of them."

"But if not by God then by who?" Sol asks, which is exasperating because isn't this the question I have just put to him? At least he seems genuinely interested now though.

"I don't know, I'm not religious, remember?"

"Then why are you here?" he asks.

Yeah. Good question.

"You want me to call him? You think I have his number?"

"Or maybe text?" I quip.

"Hah. Yes. Everything is technology these days."

"But what is your advice then?"

He fixes me now with his pale blue eyes. Our hour almost up. He continues to stare at me, his mind thinking and finally he allows himself just the faintest of smiles.

"Why the girl?" he asks.

I shake my head. "What do you mean?"

"The woman you are looking for. The homeless woman."

"Catherine?"

"Yeah, why are you looking for her?"

I breathe out heavily. Hasn't he listened to a word I've said?

He shrugs his most Jewish shrug. "And?"

"Because she is responsible."

"For what?"

For fuck sake. Judith has some explaining to do.

"Err… for saving my life?"

"Right. You think she is some kind of angel?"

"I don't know what she is. She might as well be. She did save my life. So, at the very least, I owe her a thank you. What else have I got to go on?"

He smiles again, this time more broadly.

"But why her?" he asks again.

I close my eyes with the frustration, refusing to repeat myself again.

"And you don't know where she is?"

"No, I don't."

"So, you can't ask her?"

"No, I can't."

"So, don't worry yourself with her then."

My eyes widen.

"But this started with her?"

"Oh, really?"

"Yes. Really." I snap.

"I'm not so sure that it did," he says confidently. "Think back. Why did you give her the watch?"

"I don't know, something just came over me."

"Yes, but why?"

"Because I was angry."

"Ah," he raises a finger now. "You were angry."

"Right."

"Why? Why were you angry?"

My mind scrolls back.

"Because my jeweller..."

Sol smiles broadly.

"And I am assuming that you do know where to find this jeweller?"

CHAPTER TWENTY-THREE

I leave Sol's house in something of a daze. I thank him but he seems entirely unmoved and unaware of his impact.

"Let me know?" he smiles as he closes the door behind me. I turn and skip down his drive. Even though it is very cold, I am keen to walk for a while before hailing a taxi. Winter has finally arrived with a vengeance and in time for the Christmas season.

I feel that I have reached a pivotal juncture and perhaps my last play. I am mindful to keep my hopes in check, but I fervently hope that Sol is correct and, if he is, then being unable to see the wood for the trees occurs to me since Maurice Cohen has been ever present and yet revisiting him never once occurred to me unless to fire bomb his shop. It could be that Maurice is yet another blind alley and what then, I ask myself? Go back further in the chain, to Bella? But I can't think like this. It is too negative. There is so much is riding on my nemesis.

Returning to his shop is fraught with danger and it frightens me. He might humiliate me again or worse, and more likely, prove to be just another dead end. No answers, no kindness, no empathy or understanding, and so, I dither back and forth between going or not.

Back at my hotel, I re-read the last third of my book again and, as always, I make additions and edits. It occurs to me that a book is something that is never really ever finished but that the author eventually, just has to let go of. The passage on Troy stands out. It is most vivid, heartfelt and evocative. I recall his smell and the laughs we shared. What an evening we had. It was more fun even than my superb meal I shared with two financiers - offering me many millions of pounds, too - in a comfortable Park Lane restaurant. I recall Troy so fondly. No doubt he is through his cigarettes already and has spent the money that the Fifty Guy gave him. This thought makes me smile. I have not been out as the Fifty Guy since, too preoccupied with my own preservation.

I come to the end of the document and with it comes my familiar sense of emptiness at what remains missing. The vertical cursor is flashing at me. The keyboard remains willing, able and available. My machine has stacks of memory left. And yet, I don't feel so tortured by it anymore - probably because now I might have a way forward. It is the 18th December and a busy time for the shops and especially a jeweller. Perhaps not a good time then to call in on my least favourite retailer? He will be busy with Christmas trade. It is a bad idea to go now; I should wait until January. Yes, that makes sense. But then, what if he has a January sale? And what happened to forcing the issue and not kicking cans down metaphorical roads? Across the mouse pad, I scroll back through my document to my encounter with Maurice.

I read it slowly, imagining every moment that I describe with my words. My mouth dries instantly as I remember the intensity of each emotion: indignation, anger, hurt, alarm and surprise. My feeling of impotence and dizziness when I was jettisoned from his shop. My mind was a mess. I breathe out heavily as I finish the passage. It is just a few pages, not even three thousand words, and yet they have had such a bearing on where I am now. I begin to prevaricate again, recalling how I once felt before I gave a speech at a medical conference in Las

Vegas. In the enormous auditorium were two thousand eminent physicians and another thousand or so big hitters from big pharma. For days before my speech I felt sick with anxiety; panic-stricken at being judged and assessed by my peers. But that was nothing to how I feel now. The prospect of confronting a humble shop keeper of a second-hand jewellers is far worse.

But I think it is better to go in mid-January, once the sales are over and everything has quietened down. That makes eminent sense.

CHAPTER TWENTY-FOUR

I am in Portman Square again, sitting on my bench but now with zero expectations of Catherine's arrival. I think of her less now. If anything, I feel affronted that she should remain so removed and aloof, leaving me to flounder at the terrifying prospect of revisiting Maurice Cohen; something I must not delay any longer, I assure myself. Force the issue. Make things happen. I stand up and instantly my mouth is dry and my knees feel weak.

Later, in my viewing room, the joy of being surrounded by my treasure has still not returned. I am unsure whether this is a good thing. Today, though, I am much more purposeful. I do not bother with my audit and I will not need the full hour that I have booked. I empty a few tubes of gold coins into my hand but nothing else before returning them. I consider my Patek Phillipe watch, the jewel in my crown and the reason for my visit. A peace offering? I feel embarrassed now that I have never even worn it. How pathetic. I look at the digital clock on the wall. It is a little after 1pm, which I expect is the busiest time for Maurice at his shop. More procrastination because it is surely more sensible to aim for the shoulder of the day. An hour before closing-time seems right to me. But then what time does he shut during the festive period? Five, six, seven? I fidget with my belongings, aware that my dithering is pathetic because I have a nagging feeling that time is against me.

In Selfridges, I finish my beef sandwich and contemplate the time again, and what the next hour might have in store for me. Answers, hopefully, and some solace. I open my mouth wide and stretch my jaw and lips and go over once again what I plan to say. To begin with, I will apologise. Christ, if I can get the words out, that is. This is why I have eaten already, since I know that for such a task I will need to summon huge amounts of energy.

I walk slowly to the Burlington Arcade, delaying the inevitable and playing over in my mind my words and trying to calm myself. My mobile rings and I clutch at it, hoping it might be a worthwhile distraction, but it is just one of these blasted phishing calls about an accident that I have not been involved in. How naïve some people must be? I take a little comfort in the fact that however exploitative my medical practice is, I am far more dignified than the bottom feeding lawyers and insurance 'professionals' at work.

While taking a meandering route along Jermyn Street, I notice a homeless person sitting outside the tiny theatre. He looks to be a man in his mid-fifties but he might well be much younger; something I have learnt from experience since my reprieve. In my pocket I have a set of new fifties and I am tempted to sit with him. It might give me the encouragement and sense of virtue to take with me to see Cohen. He turns and catches my attention, his face imploring. Damn it. I want to sit with him but I need to get going and I feel a sudden urge to get moving. As I pass him, I look directly at him to apologise. Perhaps I will return after my meeting, depending on how it goes of course. He bids me farewell and I hope that he might understand that I am in crisis too. But I need to get to the shop now. I don't know why. I just have a feeling and, as I round the corner, I even break into a gentle run. Time is against me.

The famous arcade is busier than normal but this is no surprise and I try to calm myself. I feel for my Patek watch. Nice and easy, nothing to worry about. I hear lots of American accents from people peering into various shop windows. A Japanese couple are shown out of another jewellery shop, the lady with an enormous smile on her face. The jeweller thanks them and smiles too, only more obsequiously.

I sidle towards Maurice's shop, now sick with nerves. My mouth is dry and my palms are clammy. At first, I walk straight past and glance briefly into the window as I pass. I imagine that Maurice is permanently waiting for my return so that he is ready to dispatch me again at a moment's notice.

I don't see anyone inside the shop, but the display windows are designed to be looked at, not through. I carry on walking until I exit the arcade completely. The fresh, cold air is welcome because I am giddy now, just as I felt after my last visit. And still I am compelled by this pressing need for urgency and to not delay any longer. Right on cue, another tramp shuffles into view. On to set, as it were, because everything before me feels like a movie that is being directed by someone other than me.

'Cue Tramp… and, Action.'

I re-enter the arcade. I must do this now. I am going to see Maurice Cohen. I have no other options.

CHAPTER TWENTY-FIVE

I ring the bell and wait. I can't see Maurice. Hopping from foot to foot, I bite my inner lip to try and stimulate some saliva. Nothing. The door is opened by the same young sales assistant as the last time. I can see that he recognises me, but he steps aside to let me in. At least that means I am not banned.

He gestures to the couple he is already serving and I nod. No doubt, Maurice knows I am here already through his CCTV, but he does not appear and might not for a while, preferring to let me sweat. Or worse still, to let his junior assistant serve me. The couple seem to be concluding their transaction which is good news. They are both smiling broadly. Whatever they have bought, it must be perfect. Good for them.

"So, there is no sales tax that we can reclaim?" the man asks, a tall American with neat grey hair and an easy tan.

"No sir. No VAT I'm afraid with pre-owned merchandise."

"Okay, that's fine."

"I'm just so excited to have found one," the lady gushes. "It's what I have always wanted and they are so rare."

"They are indeed. We certainly get very few of them."

"I couldn't believe you had it."

She is a regal and elegant lady. The man smiles as he hands

over his black card and I continue to wait, any moment expecting Maurice to shuffle into view.

As a distraction I peer into the display cabinets but I am too stressed to take in any of the contents. It's of no interest anyway. They will be watches and diamond rings that I couldn't possibly put a value on. What trust we invest in jewellers since a diamond might well be just a lump of glass. The labels state the carat but do any of us know any better? Does anyone bring their own scales? And still, Maurice fails to show, increasing my anxiety and my humiliation. I should have planned for this contingency. It is the height of rudeness - especially since I am here on a peace mission.

The man's credit card is approved and it is handshakes all round.

"We have an appointment with a tailor on Bond Street. Could we leave this with you and pick it up later?" the man asks.

"Yes, of course. We are open until seven this evening, but someone will be here up until eight."

"No, no, we won't be long. An hour or so. Probably less."

"No problem at all, sir."

They leave the shop and the assistant makes to put the item in the safe, or perhaps back in its cabinet.

"Is Maurice here?" I ask rather tersely, unable to disguise my ire.

"No, he's not."

His answers rocks me. What? But Maurice is always here. It's Christmas. Even in august, Maurice is always in his flipping shop. And now on the day that I pluck up the courage to return, he has the temerity to have a day off? Where the fuck is he?

"Excuse me," the assistant says, "I just need to pop this back in our window."

"You mean he's popped out for lunch?" I ask hopefully, which is equally ridiculous since Maurice doesn't do lunch. He is a packed lunch man.

The assistant re-locks the internal grill to the window

display and finally offers me his full attention.

"No, he's just not in today."

"What? What do you mean?" I ask, aware of how rude I appear.

"He's having a day off," The assistant adds testily.

"A day off?" I repeat.

The man doesn't reply, just turns his head and widens his eyes. Yes, pal. Maurice is not in. Get over it.

"Is there anything I can help with?"

"No. I need to see Maurice."

"Well, like I say…"

"When is he back?"

The man chuckles a little at this. "Possibly tomorrow."

Possibly? Jesus Christ. What the fuck is going on here?

"Maurice has some family matters to attend to," the assistant offers to shut me down. I look at him curiously.

"Family matters?" I ask.

"Yes, I believe so. Matters of a personal nature," he says quietly. In other words, don't ask.

"Right, well I am a friend of Maurice…"

An eyebrow rises at this.

"…and it is critical that I see him. So, is there any chance that you might call him?"

"No."

"No?"

"Yes, that's right. Mr. Cohen is not to be disturbed. I have just made the best sale we have made all year and I am not even phoning him with the news." He gestures to the window cabinet for good measure.

"Right, well he'll be in a good mood then?" I joke, since we both know that Maurice is rarely in a good mood. He doesn't laugh.

"So, you won't call him then?" I ask.

"No. I will not."

I glare at the insolent young man.

"Maurice is spending time with his daughter and he does not want to be disturbed."

Damn it. This could not work out any worse for me. I have ceded the advantage of surprise and now that he knows I wish to meet him, he has the power to simply refuse.

The assistant makes a gesture which clearly indicates that he has work to do and could I please leave.

"Hang on, wait."

"Yes," he answers heavily.

"His daughter?"

He eyes me carefully and takes a beat. Suddenly he looks a little sheepish and less sure of himself.

"Yes."

"But Maurice doesn't have a daughter."

He waits again, as though considering his options.

"Yes, he does now."

Bloody hell. I shake my head in frustration. The randy old goat, it's a wonder that his wife was still able to conceive.

"I will tell him that you popped in again."

Yes, you do that, pal.

"Yes, thank you. And please tell him that it was not to have something valued."

"I will, indeed. When I see him next?"

I feel my Patek again but don't bother to reveal it.

"When?" I ask. "When will you see him, next? It's just that it's important."

The man sighs.

"Tomorrow?" I ask.

"I don't know, maybe tomorrow, yes. Maurice is off work a lot these days."

Really? What the hell could be keeping this old work horse away from his wretched shop? Not a new-born, surely? Not when it's his sixth!

"And you won't phone him?" I ask again. "I'm sorry to be persistent. Perhaps I could leave my number?"

"Fine." He angrily retrieves a pad and paper and I scribble down my number. He sees me out without either of us saying another word.

Outside the shop, I stand to one side so that I am obscured by his displays and so he can't see me. With my back to the glass, I exhale heavily and make a quick assessment. Certainly, I have lost any advantage I had. What a confusing exchange and set of circumstances. Altogether, odd. A Japanese couple are trying to take in the window display but I am obscuring their view.

"Oh, I am sorry."

As I move aside, I turn to face the shop also and something catches my eye. The couple crowd the window front, now blocking my view, and so rudely I barge between them. The man is aghast and tuts loudly but I don't care as I stare through the glass of Maurice's shop.

In the display, front and centre, is a ladies watch. It is atop a tall plinth beneath a dedicated light and with a neat SOLD sign beneath. An Audemars Piguet, of which there must be many thousands in the world, but no matter; I have seen this watch before because it used to be mine. I stare at the small timepiece. It is brilliant on its tiny stage, as though it is enjoying the limelight. It is Bella's watch. I know it. And the implications of seeing it in Maurice's shop window sends my mind spinning.

My mind races and scrambles as I try to make sense of what is before me. My heart beating fast to keep up with my adrenal gland, I ring on the bell incessantly, knocking also for good measure. The assistant's face falls when he spots me. This guy, again. Through the door, he calls loudly.

"What?" He mouths.

"Just open the bloody door!"

As soon as he does, I am upon him immediately and completely frantic, because the watch can only mean one thing.

"I've just spoken to Maurice..."

Oh, really? So, you lied? But that is unimportant now.

"That watch in the window. The AP. It's mine."

His face fills with horror. Never mind calling Maurice again, he might need to call the police. Beneath the counter is a panic button just in case.

"How dare you. That piece is sold."

"Yes, I know it's sold. I can see that. But its mine."

His eyes narrow now.

"I think you should leave."

"What? No way. Not this time. When did it come in, the watch?"

He raises a finger and shakes his head.

"That is classified information which you have no right to ask for."

"It was May this year, wasn't it? Or just after, in June?"

His eyes widen just a little.

"I am not obliged to answer any of your questions…"

"Can I see it?"

"No, you certainly cannot. It is sold."

"No, but you don't understand," I plead.

"Get out of this shop. If you do not leave then I will call security."

Still frantic, my mind still racing, I test different hypotheses and possibilities, always reverting to my original hope and theory.

"His daughter!" I exclaim.

"Please leave or I will call the police."

I laugh now, confident that I am right.

"Maurice is with his daughter." I state.

"Yes, that's right. Now get out."

"What's her name?"

"Last chance, get out."

"Catherine? It's Catherine, isn't it?"

His face falls.

He doesn't need to reply or say anything at all – the answer is clearly written on his face. I start to weep. Maurice is not at home attending to a new baby daughter. How could I have been so slow? His wife is in her fifties, got to be. Catherine is his new daughter because she used to be his son. In my mind's eye, I see Catherine's happy and smiling face. Her boyish good looks. The young woman who saved my life and, in doing so, forged a new bond with her old man who was struggling to accept her. Why else would he not be at work?

I stumble back and steady myself as my knees almost buckle. Even the incalcitrant assistant seems to sense something momentous is happening. He has, at least, stopped asking me to leave. I smile. I can finish my book now. All this time the answers have been right there, in plain sight. I will see Catherine again after all, but when she is ready and with my friend's blessing, Maurice Cohen. Everything happens for a reason and never before in my life have I been happier.

"Would you call Maurice, please."

The assistant nods and reaches for the phone.

"If you tell him that it is Gabriel Webber and I have some rather extraordinary and wonderful news to share with him and his beautiful daughter."

At the door now is the American couple, returning to retrieve their watch. What fortunate timing; a fraction later and I might have missed it and my life and story would never have completed.

"I need to deal with these customers," the sales assistant says.

"Yes, of course."

"But you'll call Maurice?"

"I will, absolutely, at the very first opportunity."

"Good, thank you."

I need to get back to Jermyn Street. There's a man outside the theatre I would like to speak to.

The End

OTHER BOOKS BY DOMINIC HOLLAND:

Only in America

The story of *Only in America* was inspired from my experiences with my first ever screenplay, *The Faldovian Club*. And with success of this novel, *Only in America*, my adventures in Hollywood would continue and my ill-fated forays to LA underpins the story of my only work of non-fiction, *Eclipsed.*

"This book is so charming and funny. A genuine page turner, I read it on holiday and missed big chunks of Venice"

Sandi Toksvig

"A fine stand-up comic has turned in to a first class, laugh out loud novelist. Read and enjoy"

Barry Cryer

"The only book I have ever read in one sitting. Of all the books by comedians turning their hands to novel writing - this is the funniest, most enjoyable and satisfying"

Nottingham Post

"As soon as you pick it up, you forget about everything that you have you to do, and you read it from cover to cover and you laugh out loud and love it."

Jenny Hanley

"Witty and charming. Astonishingly good. Quite irritating in fact."

Angus Deayton

"…of all the comedians turning their hands to novel writing – including Stephen Fry – this is the funniest, most enjoyable and satisfying."

Nottingham Post

"Holland's novel is witty, warm, enjoyable, addictive, captivating and hilariously funny. Laughing out loud on your own can be an unnerving experience, but laugh uncontrollably I did."

Oxford Mail

Open Links

This book was written for the Anthony Nolan Trust - the largest bone barrow register in the world. Anthony Nolan saves many hundreds of lives each year. All monies from this book go to this charity in the hope that somewhere, sometime, someone with blood cancer will be tissue matched and a chance that their life can be saved. By buying *Open Links*, you will be contributing to this noble effort. Thank you.

"From the first page I was gripped, and delighted to be reading a 'can't put this down' book. The story was funny and inspiring, the warm characters formed clear pictures in my head and the writing flowed effortlessly without a dull moment. There were several laugh out loud moments, and I have to admit an occasional tear."

"...a seriously good read... making it very hard to put down and always a case of "Just one more chapter..."

"Mr. Holland will take you on the most entertaining and heart-tugging "round" of your life"

"Like the best underdog tales, this builds momentum beautifully and has a heart of gold"

"This is a genuinely touching story that had me thinking "just one more hole" each time I picked it up. A great read and an even better cause"

"Genuinely one of the funniest and most heart-warming books I have read in years"

"This story has it all, and caught me where it counts in the "big picture" department. A great story with an even greater cause. Books like this are written from a deep place to do true good in the world. What more can you say?"

A Man's Life

This novel began its life as a screenplay called *The Fruit Bowl* and like *Only in America* played an integral role in my story, *Eclipsed.* I did manage to sell the screenplay and it was nearly set up as a film on two occasions before it eventually perished and why I decided to write the story in to a novel. It is available only as an eBook (at present) and even though I did have it professionally copy edited, I am weary of being scolded for its typos. I have given it another pass but I suspect that some remain - so my apologies.

'Within three chapters I was hooked and distraught as the story unfolded and then intrigued as we moved into the plot. I couldn't put it down, really wanted to know how it ended and am a little bereft now I've finished."

"Quite simply one of the best books I have read! Very much in the John O'Farrell mould - only better - how on earth someone hasn't turned this into a film I just don't know. I have re-read the final couple of chapters a few times as they are simply wonderful"

"What an enjoyable book. I am sitting here a 1.30am feeling a little lost because I have finished this book. You know that sad empty feeling when something great is over"

"Having read his two previous books, The Ripple Effect *and* Only in America *(both of which I'd strongly urge you to check out and buy as well), over the last few years I always kept an eye out on Amazon for his next offering. Finally I managed to find* A Man's Life *and bought it without hesitation. I wasn't disappointed"*

"It is extremely rare that I write a review of a book but on this occasion, I feel that it is necessary and hope that it will help to spread the word of this excellent author and comedian"

"Equally as good as The Ripple Effect *and* Only in America *(both of which I would also recommend)"*

The Ripple Effect

My second published novel (and last!) Currently, available as an eBook only and not available in any good book shops.

I do have plans to create a print book version but the list is long…

"A joyous romp - The Ripple Effect is an Ealing comedy for the 21st Century"

Alan Coren

"Only in America was a step in the right direction, but The Ripple Effect heralds Holland's emergence in to the literary big time."

The Sunday Times

"Proof that Holland is a master of comedy"

Northern Echo

"A belter of a novel. This could be the book of the season."

Danny Baker

"Funny, gripping and hard to put down – what more do you want from a novel?"

The Sunday Times

"An infectious, warm-hearted tale about real people pulling together."

The Mirror

"Not every stand-up comedian manages to be as funny in print as they are on stage. Dominic Holland is one of the few who is."

Liverpool Daily Post

"Proof that Holland is a master of comedy."

Yorkshire Evening Press

Eclipsed

The story of two men and their ambitions to break Hollywood; one as a writer and the other as an actor. The writer is a deluded dad called Dominic and the actor is his eldest son, called Tom.

It is now 2019 and Dominic Holland has yet to hear that seductive word, 'Action'. Tom, meanwhile, is Spider-Man with Hollywood at his beck and call, hence the title of the book, Eclipsed - a heartfelt and funny story on fatherhood written by a dad who is as bemused as he is proud.

"One might think this is a selfish attempt to gain fame and fortune at the expense of his son. This is the not the case. Eclipsed is written with more brutal honesty and self-deprecating humour than can be expected from anyone with selfish intentions"

"Dominic Holland bravely exposes his hopes and disappointments, his talents and his frailties in a story which is ultimately redemptive in its fearless honesty and open-hearted spirit. 'Eclipsed' is a bitter-sweet tale of great liveliness and warmth; above all, it is profoundly human"

"Dominic Holland doesn't claim 'superior genes', 'unique talent' or 'fate' for his son Tom, but gives credit to his hard work, application and a high degree of natural talent. This is a truly remarkable, balanced perspective given the dizzy heights to which Tom's career has already achieved and which have so far eluded his old man"

"Whilst the context for Eclipsed is unique, the themes of parental love, pride, self-esteem versus self-doubt and the sense of handing the baton on to the next generation are universal. For any parent who has ever let their child beat them in a running race to encourage them when they were young, only to have them sail past you leaving you panting in their wake once they come of age, this book will resonate strongly. It is funny, fast-paced, moving and uplifting in equal measure. And at the heart of the story is the belief that hope will triumph over most things"

"I loved this book as it's funny, honest and heartfelt. My kind of book. Any parent could relate to this and at times it felt like I was reading the script of a movie. I hope you enjoy it, I did"

"Dominic's style is funny, candid, engaging and honest. The way he describes the scenes and events is hilarious and at times I sat on the train laughing out loud. I recommend it to all twenty first century parents"

Dominic is very grateful to those readers who write reviews of his books for the various websites which might help sales and reverse his Eclipse!

Dominic writes a regular blog (and has plans for a podcast) and can be found at www.dominicholland.co.uk

Of particular interest on this site might be "Book a show near you" – your chance for Dominic to arrive at your venue, school, pub, theatre for a full one man show and or a book reading. Despite his continued and best efforts, Dominic does not appear on TV anymore, so you will need to provide the audience and he will take care of the rest. Promise!